ROLLING HOME

A Novel

Austin Charters

ROLLING HOME
Copyright © 2018 by Austin Charters

First Printing, 2018
ISBN 978-1-7324093-1-6 (Paperback)

Stay in touch with the author:

www.C5Roller.com
Instagram – @C5Roller
www.Facebook.com/C5Roller

Formatting by: The Book Khaleesi
www.thebookkhaleesi.com

10 9 8 7 6 5 4 3 2 1

To Grandpa Jack and Ryan Charters: The reason I live. The reason I laugh. The reason I love. Without you, there would be no me. Without you, I wouldn't have the strength to carry on. You saved my life, and for that, I am forever grateful. A simple dedication does not make up for everything I owe the both of you.

To Mom and Dad: Thank you for keeping me grounded. You helped shape and mold me into the person I am today. You are the epitome of everything I am. It goes without saying, but you both are the best things I have in my life. Nothing could ever come close to explaining my love and appreciation for you.

To Owen, John, Ben, Damian and Johnny: My extended brothers. Your friendship is my most valued treasure. Through thick and thin you all have been by my side cheering me on. I couldn't ask for a more perfect family.

RIP KC66

I love you all dearly!

PROLOGUE

Falling

It's like Alice in Wonderland.

I'm going down the rabbit hole. In the story, I remember Alice falling forever. Just when it seemed like she would come in for a landing...there'd be nothing to catch her but more open space.

Tumbling, toppling...into eternity...

What just happened to me?

My mind's not working properly. I can see the warm sun hanging in the sky. I can remember the look on my grandpa's face.

And the gun in his hand.

A little curl of smoke rising up from its snout.

Then, for a fraction of a second, before I began to tumble, there was that look on his face. It told me many things. (Tumbling, toppling...) It told me something had gone very, very wrong. (...into eternity.)

It told me things would never be the same.

CHAPTER 1

Packing

T uckeeeeerrrrrr!"
It was my mother's voice. It went all the way up my spine. Nothing was wrong – I could tell she wasn't mad or anything – but still, when she had to call me from downstairs, she pushed it just a little too hard, and I'd feel her sound registering in all my nerve endings.

"What?!" I yelled, my eyes fixed on my giant overnight bag, which was spread across half the surface of my mattress and stuffed with way more things than I'd ever need for a three-night camping trip: too many changes of clothes (among them way too many pairs of socks), a big mess of snacks (half of which were chocolate, and would probably melt within a couple hours), a roll of quarters (for no reason whatsoever), a canteen, a flashlight, the hunting vest my grandpa had bought for me a year before, and a bunch of sports and outdoors magazines that I had virtually no chance of getting around to reading. After all, on every trip my family went on, I always brought a lot of reading material, but somehow it always managed to stay untouched. There was always way too much to do, and too much tiredness in my bones when it was finally bedtime.

This particular trip wasn't a "family" outing in the strictest sense. My mom and dad weren't coming along. Neither was my Grandma Hazel. No, this time out, it'd be me, my older brother Jordan, and my Grandpa Angus.

The legendary Angus.

Grandpa Angus had the one ingredient that was missing from my overnight bag, the one thing I, as a teenager, could not be entrusted with carrying:

The firearms.

And when my mother called me from downstairs, rattling my spine and telling me – after I answered her with no shortage of irritation – that "somebody was here" to see me, I was all but positive that Grandpa Angus had arrived. Sure, he was 90 minutes early, but then again, this was an important trip. We'd gone hunting plenty of times before, but never in as remote an area, and definitely never overnight. But with Columbus Day weekend now on top of us, giving me a much-needed break early on in my junior year, we finally had a chance to do some serious hunting. In all likelihood, we'd probably go after birds and small mammals like squirrels and rabbits. But up in Mount Radiance, where we'd be camping, there were also known to be plenty of deer, and even some bears if you got lucky.

Or *unlucky*, rather. To be honest, I kind of went in hoping that we wouldn't run into any bears...

In a subtle way, my heartbeat had started pumping faster. It wasn't that aggressive, rat-a-tat-tat kind of pump I felt after running or even riding on a motorbike; it was driven more by anticipation than adrenaline. 'Cause right now, downstairs, the big man was waiting. I couldn't yet make out his voice, but I knew he was down there, in all his glory, waiting to take his grandkids out on one hell of a hunt.

Grandpa Angus. The one and only.

And I always looked forward to seeing him...

* * *

My Grandpa Angus wasn't your typical man's man. He was more...sensitive...in a way – yeah, I guess that's the word I'm looking for. You looked in his eyes and you could see all the way to his heart. I kind of liked to think of myself that way, whenever I looked at myself in the mirror. He was a *soulful* guy; his face belonged in the dictionary beside that word. When he laughed, it came from a deep, true place. When he spoke to you, he did so with sincerity and simplicity.

AUSTIN CHARTERS

I always had to remind myself to not make too much of the guy. After all, whether he was my grandfather or not, he was still just a man – no more, no less. But he struck me as the kind of man who had happened upon answers to some of life's most serious questions. I'm not saying he'd discovered the meaning of life or anything like that, but just that he'd figured out how to live. He moved with ease. He took pleasure wherever he could find it, but never at anyone else's expense.

And I loved him completely, as did Jordan. Though I can't speak for Jordan, I feel pretty confident in saying that Grandpa Angus was the first man I ever knew I loved. I mean, I love my father, Mike, as well, but he's a complicated man, and therefore, when it comes to him, I feel a kind of complicated love.

* * *

He was out in the hallway when I was born.

My father, I mean.

That almost makes it worse than if he had actually been far away. Like, if he'd been out of town then that would be understandable. But no: my dad was right there, like 20 feet away, in the hospital corridor when I came into the world.

The reason? He'd been pounding a few too many shots. I was born in the evening, after his work shift and before his supper.

Right in that two-hour window when he could be counted on to hit the bars.

And the nurses could see right through his facade; at least that's the way my mother relayed the story to me. He'd tried for half an hour to convince everybody that he was okay. More than okay, in fact: actually capable of being useful when it came to delivering his second son. But they weren't buying it. They smelled the liquor right there on top of his lies. And before long they figured this guy was taking up too much space.

So to the hallway he went. Sat on a chair. Leaving my mother to do it alone (or only with the staff members).

I sometimes wonder whether he even thought about me out there in the hall. Was his mind in connection with the reality around him, or was he sailing away down some drunken river, dreaming of the life he'd once imagined for himself but never claimed?

A life where he drove expensive cars rather than just selling them.

A life where he had more savings than debt.

A life where his first son, who was almost three at the time, ran into his arms before seeking out the arms of his wife's father, Angus.

Who could say?

It's impossible to ever really know what my dad is thinking. I mean, I've had my share of deep discussions with him, and he's more or less accessible about half the time, but that doesn't mean you're getting his authentic self.

To be honest, I'm not even sure if *he* ever gets his authentic self.

'Cause that self seems like a pretty angry guy.

The kind he'd like to keep tucked away under layers of liquor.

In fact, while growing up, I came to see him as a guy who was always out in the hall – not just literally on my first day of life, but symbolically, on an ongoing basis.

Even when he was standing right there in front of you, there was always a pretty strong possibility that he was actually very far away.

* * *

Which of course made it all the more refreshing to see Grandpa Angus.

In fact, over the years I began to wonder whether Grandpa at some point started modeling his personality to be different from my dad's. Where dad was absent, Grandpa was present. Where dad was aloof, Grandpa was available.

Where dad was drunk, Grandpa was sober.

The two men actually liked each other. I can't recall a single instance when either one criticized the other behind his back, much less spoke a single ill word of the other. On the contrary, they were known to engage in easy banter, giving each other their space and even being able to share unforced, casual laughs.

I suppose it was easier to like my dad if you didn't have to live with him.

Anyway, living with him was off the table for the weekend. I'd said goodbye to him the night before, knowing that he'd still be working at the dealership when Grandpa picked me up after school, so I didn't have to worry about running into him until Monday night, after we were home again.

And though I hated to admit it to myself, that made me excited. Freedom was near, now. A weekend of being able to act just like myself.

Though when I reached the bottom of the steps, I got an inkling deep in the fibers of my gut that this weekend might not turn out to be so exciting after all.

'Cause instead of Grandpa Angus standing there – being the "someone" who my mom said was here to see me – it was my best friend, Mikey Carmichael, a.k.a. Double Mike.

* * *

We called him Double Mike because his name, Mikey Carmichael, had a pair of Mikes inside it. The nickname worked well enough; he was the kind of guy who deserved a nickname: colorful, outgoing, made friends easily. I was on the more shy side. Though I had a bunch of friends and had dated a few girls, it was clear when I was next to Mikey that he was the more talkative one.

But the tradeoff was that I was the one who drew in the interest of girls.

Maybe they liked me 'cause I was more quiet, and they wanted to know what I was thinking. Or maybe they just thought I was good-looking, like my mom always insisted I was. In any event, Double Mike and I had a system where he'd take me around to public places – like parks or malls or even afterschool games – and invite girls to come and sit with us.

One look at Double Mike, and they weren't so sure.

One look at me, though, and they decided to give us a shot.

Anway, Mike did most of the talking. I chimed in here or there for a joke or two, which the girls could usually be relied upon to laugh at. So when Mikey showed up at my house that Friday afternoon, I guessed correctly that he wanted to "work the system", as we called it.

There was a party coming up that night, and Mikey was pissed at me for the fact that I was going out of town.

"I can't just cancel it," I said. "We've planned it for six weeks."

"How do you plan a thing like this for six weeks? You're just going up to shoot a bunch of animals."

I gave him a smile. "Yeah, good thing you're not coming. You'd blow your own foot off."

He shook his head. He wasn't game for laughing.

ROLLING HOME

We were standing on my driveway, out in the modest, late-fall heat, and he took a look around the cul-de-sac where my family's house was located, as though in search of an answer to his predicament.

I patted his shoulder. "You'll be fine. What the hell do you even need me for?"

He looked at me again. Didn't have to say it. It was me who broke the eye contact this time.

"Look," I said, "I gotta go."

"Where? Your grandpa's not even here yet."

I made a big display of pulling out my bike from the open garage. "I'm going over to his place. Help him pack."

A giant sigh came out of Double Mike's mouth. How he even could have expected his little begging and pleading routine to turn out successfully was beyond me. I mean, he was a manipulative cat, no doubt about it, and really good when it came to talking himself, or both of us, out of trouble.

But nothing was going to get in the way of my coming weekend.

"See ya on Tuesday," I said, as I biked away.

"Yeah, whatever. You suck."

I biked on, shaking my head.

"Talk later!" Double Mike called after me.

'Cause he always liked to end things on a peaceful note.

* * *

What I love about my Grandpa is that he didn't even comment on my sudden appearance. He actually never found out that I'd biked to his house just to avoid the annoying and uncomfortable chat with Double Mike. When I pulled up his driveway and found him loading up his SUV, he acted as though we'd planned it that way all along.

"Your grandmother's worried about bears," he said, instead of saying hello.

We shook hands. I patted the rear of his shoulder. We weren't much for hugging, which was probably a habit left over from his generation. Just the same, a handshake from him was way warmer than a hug from my dad.

"I'm worried about bears, too," I said, laughing – and happy that my grandma had given me an opening to say so.

He shot me a sharp look. A glint of amusement came from his eye. Without opening his mouth, he seemed to say, *"What are you, a pansy?"*

I just laughed again.

"Well, Tucker," he said, putting a great hand on my shoulder, "bears do have claws, and SIZE, and very sharp teeth. But you know what they don't have?"

I shrugged.

He whispered, leaning in close, "Guns."

Now it was me who shook my head. "Yeah," I said, "good luck drawing a gun when a bear pulls your tent off you at three a.m."

"Ha! Don't have to draw it." He winked at me. "It'll be in my hand."

We laughed together.

Grandma Hazel stepped out the front door, holding a small duffle bag from underneath rather than by the handle, as though it were a cake on a platter.

"This is the last of it," she said.

She meant the luggage, but I kind of sensed on some level she was saying this would be Grandpa Angus's last hunting trip. She complained every time he went away on these things. And now that he'd be bringing her two grandbabies with him...it was a violation beyond her comprehension.

"Thanks, sweetie," Grandpa said.

With a nod, Grandma Hazel stuffed the sack into the open trunk. Then Grandpa slammed it. She looked at me, as unsurprised as he'd been by my presence: "You gonna put your bike on the roof?" she asked me.

I looked at it. I of course hadn't planned for getting it home.

"Nah," Grandpa said, lifting my bike off the driveway and wheeling it toward his garage. "He'll pick it up next week. Let's go, kiddo. Get your brother."

"Okay." I curved around to the passenger side door.

"Aren't you forgetting something?" my grandma asked me.

Without missing a beat, I went over to her and gave her a kiss on the cheek. The mixed scent of powder and perfume filled my nose. It briefly brought me back to the time when I was little.

Something grabbed my heart as she and I said goodbye. By then, I had drifted away from my center. Things didn't feel right. The sun seemed slanted in the sky. Everything in my world was a little bit doomy. Sure, I was a moody teenager, and could go from high to low in a split second, but this was different.

Something was in the air.

It had started when I saw Double Mike. His presence had seemed dream-like, like he wasn't really Double Mike, but just a hologram version of himself.

Maybe he'd been sent there to give me a message.

Maybe his begging and pleading hadn't been so strange after all.

Maybe some force was warning me not to go on this trip.

* * *

My emotions didn't get any lighter during the two-minute car ride from my grandparents' house to my house.

For it was during that car ride when Grandpa Angus told me a piece of information that seemed trivial in the moment but would later amount to the biggest life change I'd ever experienced.

"Shoot," he said, his jaw clenching as he pulled up to a red light.

"What?" I asked him.

Shaking his head and sighing – as though the first action permitted the second – he said, "I left my holster in the shed. Damn it."

"Wanna turn around? It's three blocks."

"Nah," he said, shaking his head again. "No big deal. I'll just keep it in my pocket. Will be fine."

It's funny, in retrospect, how clearly I remember the first word of his last sentence: "will."

Not "we'll."

Will.

Be fine.

But for a moment there I heard it as "we'll."

Because by then I was kind of worried about all of us.

CHAPTER 2

Shooting

We were in the woods for less than two hours when all hell broke loose.

Jordan drove Grandpa's SUV up to Mount Radiance. There was some tension between them along the way, for even though Jordan had got his driver's license almost four years ago, in Grandpa's world he was still just a new driver. Add to this the complexity and danger of navigating the mountain ride, and by the time we finally reached the camping site, the two of them were well on top of each other's nerves.

"We gonna hunt first or pitch the tent?" Jordan asked Grandpa, in a tone that got across that he wanted to move on with the trip yet was still pretty irritated from the ride.

"Pitch the tent."

So the three of us started unwrapping the tent supplies. It was a quiet, physical, manly stretch of time, with us handing each other items absent any conversation or affection. The moment, however, got interrupted when a streak of motion tore across the woods.

Grandpa, who had been down in a crouch, stood upright.

Jordan followed. I stood up third, with one word shrieking across the expanse of my mental landscape: *BEAR!*

"What was that?" Jordan asked Grandpa. Whatever attitude he'd had before was gone.

"Not sure."

Grandpa lit out toward the foliage. Maintaining the order in which we rose, Jordan took off running after him, leaving me alone at the camp site for a moment. I felt my blood rush through my veins. No part of me wanted to follow those two.

But even less of me wanted to be all alone.

So I followed them. When I got to the patch of forest where they stood, Grandpa had his rifle in aim and was hurrying after the massive, hulking, muscular source of the sound:

It was a deer.

I sighed. *Phew.* That I could handle.

Next thing I knew, my feet were carrying me along behind Jordan and Grandpa. We weren't running, exactly, as that would make too many leaves crunch under us, but we were taking swift and semi-sideways steps, tracking the animal as best we could despite its pretty amazing speed.

Grandpa stopped atop a wide rock. Up ahead, the deer galloped toward a curve. This was his last chance; if the deer turned, we'd never get it back in our sight. My cheeks crunched upward. If I were a little kid, I would've stuck my fingertips in my ears.

Grandpa took aim. The deer was a hairy flash of motion.

When the gun went off, birds scattered from the trees overhead. Ironically, killing a bird would have been real easy at that moment.

But we had bigger prey in sight.

As the deer made its turn, some tree bark sprayed outward.

Grandpa had taken a nice, clean shot – after all, he was all but a pro at this – but hadn't managed to hit the animal. As it ran away, I could hear my heartbeat in my ears.

This was exciting. Hunting was fun.

With all this adrenaline in my body, I found myself looking forward to whatever was next.

* * *

The worst moment in my life happened really fast.

We were back at the camp site, in high spirits as we discussed our mini-adventure with the deer. Jordan and I assured Grandpa that he'd done as well as possible under the circumstances. Had we known of the deer's presence a moment sooner, it would have been a kill shot – no doubt about it.

Grandpa shrugged his shoulders, unsure. I sensed that he was logically frustrated about missing the prey, but not emotionally so. In his mind, it all came down to basic rifle logistics. He wasn't as concerned about his timing as his ability to handle the weapon. Regardless, his heart wasn't in the matter. Like, I don't think his blood was boiling; I think he was simply considering how to improve his shot the next time out.

That also struck me as a generational thing. Jordan and I were more emotional creatures. We spoke our minds, even spoke our hearts. Not all the time, but certainly more than Grandpa. At his age, though, life seemed to come down to common sense. Functional matters. If you missed the shot, you didn't bitch about missing out on your moment of glory; you simply ascertained the logical reasons as to why your attempt had failed.

However, the next time Grandpa Angus's gun went off, his reaction would no doubt be entirely emotional...

* * *

We didn't go back to pitching the tent just yet. Our blood was now running too hot for that. Accordingly, we ate some chips and sandwiches. I knew that potato chips slow people down, and I didn't want to get sluggish with the sun still so high in the sky, but chasing the deer had made me hungry. I think the electroshock of excitement in my system had eaten up a lot of my energy.

Same with the other two. It was time to refuel.

"What was the biggest animal you ever killed, Grandpa?"

This was Jordan talking.

Grandpa chewed on his salami sandwich. "It's not the size of the animal that makes the kill meaningful. It's the wits. The intelligence."

"Okay," Jordan laughed. "So that means you'd be more proud to kill a rat than an elephant? 'Cause rats are pretty clever, you know."

Grandpa and I both laughed.

"Well the truth is," Grandpa said, clarifying his previous remark, "I don't have much experience with large game. That deer back there – that would have been memorable."

"Have you ever shot a deer before?" I asked him.

He nodded. "A couple. Maybe three or four, even. It's hard to remember. Past few years, it's been mostly birds. Mostly for the sport of it. One time, though – since you asked about my biggest kill – I actually managed to take down a moose."

My eyebrows rose. Moose didn't cross my mind very much. They didn't have any (at least that I knew of) near us in Southern California.

"A moose?" I asked.

Grandpa Angus nodded. He finished his sandwich and let out a silent, clipped-off belch. Then he stood and started circling the tent gear.

"I was in Washington State," he said. "Gosh, this was back when your grandma was still pregnant with your mother. Or maybe your mom was still a little kid. I can't remember. But moose, now...those are glorious creatures. You have to have a real respect for them. The one I nabbed was giant – size of a couple refrigerators – but the speed on her..."

"It was a her?" I asked.

Nodding, he said, "Oh yeah. Magnificent. That was one hell of an outing. First I thought I hadn't hit her, 'cause there was so much fog, but then--"

* * *

But Grandpa never finished his story.

'Cause when he bent over to get back to work on the tent, the handgun he'd tucked inside his vest slipped out. See, the cloth in those vests is pretty soft. As it turned out, the gun wasn't very secure inside the pocket after all.

And when it hit the ground, it went off.

Then a bullet went through my neck as fast as lightning.

AUSTIN CHARTERS

* * *

It's like *Alice in Wonderland.*

I'm going down the rabbit hole. In the story, I remember Alice falling forever. Just when it seemed like she would come in for landing...there'd be nothing to catch her but more open space.

Tumbling, toppling...into eternity...

What just happened to me?

My mind's not working properly. I can see the warm sun hanging in the sky. I can remember the look on my grandfather's face.

And the gun in his hand.

A little curl of smoke rising up from its snout.

Then, for a fraction of a second, before I began to tumble, there was that look on his face. It told me many things. (Tumbling, toppling...) It told me something had gone very, very wrong. (...into eternity.)

It told me things would never be the same.

* * *

A burning feeling replaced my blood. I smashed into the ground. I'd later learn that my neck had broken and my spinal cord had been severed.

But for now all I knew was a world of pain.

I heard laughter, though. Not malicious – they just thought I was kidding. Playing a rapid-fire prank.

Thinking just as fast as that bullet.

But when Grandpa felt my blood on his fingers, the smile on his face ducked for cover.

"We gotta go!" he yelled to Jordan.

Jordan was quivering. *Quaking.* "Where?!"

"Ranger's station! Ten miles! Come on!"

Grandpa's mighty hands were on my calves.

"No!" shrieked Jordan. "You get the top!"

They switched places. Grandpa's hands were hooked into my armpits. Jordan scooped me up by the legs. They went running, but they didn't know where they were going. My body zigzagged this way and that.

The site we'd picked to camp at was tucked up against a hillside. The SUV had been left in a little dirt parking lot above, at the top of a 100-yard climb. Getting down the hill earlier in the day had been kind of a pain, but nothing serious.

And now they had to get up it, carrying me.

"Come on, come on, come on," Grandpa said.

I saw the sky. Its gentle blueness, so calm in theory. But that was it for me; I knew it.

I was dead.

Nothing was working. My whole being had been caved in. I tried to line up one thought behind another, but everything just kept retreating from me.

Then the ground rushed up at me: I'd been dropped.

"Pick him up, pick him up!"

"That's what I'm doing!"

"We need to go fast!"

"I'm going as fast as I can!"

With a *whish*, I'd defied gravity once again. I was back up: floating, bending, flying, *dropping--*

Fuck.

They'd done it again.

Only this time I didn't fall flat; I rolled. And as I rolled, inside my mind, I began to fall again. *Forever.* Through empty space. Total space. So much space that it was as though the concept of anything being solid had not yet been born.

Up!

Here we went. More motion. Grandpa at my calves this time. No, it was Jordan. No...

I don't know.

My skull was a constant throb.

Whole body an empty sack.

They were going as fast as they could, but getting nowhere. I tried to speak. Maybe I *was* speaking. The sky kept curving. Some birds were far away, in a world of their own.

Upward, upward, onward, we went...

Hillside almost gone, now. Car, soon. Faster, faster. Help, *help!*

No need for help...

No more *me.* Where was I?

Nowhere. Nothing.

No more hillside.

Then down again. Dropped again!

ROLLING HOME

Rolling again. Couple feet this time. Leaves and sticks all over my body. Crunches in my hair. My lungs not rising.

Blood not pumping.

Eyes granting sight to a dead, beige mind.

Then up, up, and away once again--

No more hillside. For real this time. And Grandpa's running. And Jordan's running.

The ground's more level. And I'm a rag doll.

And before I know it, a thousand years later...

There's the car.

* * *

"Tell Mom and Dad I love them."

This was me.

"You're not gonna die."

That was Jordan.

"Tell Mom and Dad I love them."

This was me, over and over again as we drove.

"I'll tell them, okay?! Just hang on, Tucker!"

Hang onto what? Nothing to hang onto.

I wasn't working, that much was clear. I had a broiling hell where my neck belonged. An ocean of numbness where my body belonged.

And a scream of terror where my mind belonged.

No way a person could get out of this. If God existed, then he hadn't been kidding around when he programmed this possibility into the machine. This was a dead end. A glimpse of true hell.

A cul-de-sac. Just like the one I'd grown up in.

Only now my growing up was over. Whole life was over. Death was – how close? Any second? Any moment?

Had it already come?

"Tell Mom and Dad I love them."

* * *

The guy at the Ranger Station's name was Milo.

"We had an accident," Grandpa Angus explained. "My gun slipped out of my jacket and hit the ground. It went off, and the bullet went through my grandson's neck."

His words were weighted down by a colossal ache.

"It broke the bone. He can't walk. We had to carry him up a hill. We need medical attention right away. Right away, do you understand? *I shot my grandson...*"

Only needless to say, that wasn't true. He hadn't shot me. He'd dropped the gun.

But in his mind, the transaction was complete: He'd transferred ownership of the incident from the gods, or the fates, or whatever you want to call them (or it) to himself.

And though I didn't know it at the time, he'd never give it back.

* * *

ROLLING HOME

Ice.

Sharp ice. Freezing ice.

Inside a blue pack against my neck.

Milo's meaty hand: tight around the pack. My lungs still elsewhere. Not rising, not falling. Not doing anything.

Yet still: Here's me. Alive and present in the world.

An ambulance roared up. I got strapped to a stretcher. Grandpa nearby. Jordan nearby. Breathing, panting. Speaking words with their breath.

Bypassing the vocal cords.

Stretcher floating along, now. Ambulance doors open. Me slid inside: like a CD into a player. Then – bam! Two doors shut.

And the siren, the siren, the siren...

Still got ears.

And the siren's inside them...

Another guy next to me. He's got my arm. My arm's a noodle. His arm's holding an IV. He's trying to take aim.

Needs a vein.

Needs a vein like I need a hopeful future.

Like I need my life back.

Takes aim. IV. Maybe *this'll* fix me.

Ambulance races.

Sirens roar.

He pricks me with the needle, but we hit a pothole.

Whole world crunches.

"SHIT!" yells the man with the needle.

AUSTIN CHARTERS

And all is black.

CHAPTER 3

Waking

T ubes. Wires. Machines. Beeps. Lights.
Small lights, though.
More darkness than light.
And people around me. But not close. Elsewhere.
Behind doors. In hallways. In other rooms.

* * *

When I woke in the hospital, it was seven days later.

I was by myself, and felt my neck locked up in a brace the size of a toilet.

Which was a fitting metaphor, given the state I was in...

I wanted to call out, wanted to *scream* out, wanted

someone to rush in and rescue me. But I didn't have the energy to make even a tiny sound.

I shut my eyes. My brain was beating.

In my head, in the darkness, I encountered a leering and hideous reality:

Even though I was still living, something was very wrong.

* * *

It was Friday the 13th, the day I woke up.

But I wasn't entirely up after that.

For another two weeks, I drifted in and out of consciousness. Whereas you might picture someone in my position strapped to a bed and screaming his guts out, the truth is they had me on such high dosages of such sedating medication that I pretty much got deleted from human life for a while there.

As I fluttered in and out, my eyelids rising and falling, I became aware of certain key pieces of information:

My neck had been broken.

My spinal cord had been severed.

I'd lost all movement from my neck down past the bottoms of my toes. All of it was now just an eternal void, as though after a certain point in my physical being, I just dropped off into nothingness.

Just like Alice in Wonderland, dropping and dropping...

(Falling and falling...)

The good news was, my arms still worked.

But my hands were gone, more or less. I mean, I could create motion in them by way of arms, but I couldn't feel my actual hands, nor move my fingers.

As for my arms themselves, they'd take some time to get going. Each day, I'd need therapy; learn how to use them.

And how to use the bathroom.

And how to sit up.

And a lady would come in and put lotion on my wound. She'd then all but dig her fingers into it, massaging the muscles around it.

Trying to turn it into something other than gruesome.

So this was my life now: learning everything all over again. Sure, it was brutal, but on the other hand I had no choice.

People have to sit up. People have to use the restroom.

Despite the new state of my body, I *had to* do these things.

So one step at a time, one moment at a time – that's what I did.

* * *

The deepest pains that greeted me weren't physical ones.

After all, when your body can't feel too much, physical pain isn't really your problem.

No, more for me were emotional pains. Social ones, to be more exact.

For example, I asked about Double Mike. I even asked about the whole crew he and I hung around with. Were they coming to visit?

Had they even called?

I remember my dad's face when I asked those questions. Right away, he got...hidden, I guess. Or he was *trying* to hide. But I could see right through his mask:

He gave me all the info I needed without saying a word.

"No, Double Mike hasn't called," he said.

"No, Double Mike will never call," he continued.

"No, none of the guys you two hung around with are ever going to check in with you again," he capped it off with.

Again: he said all these things without ever once opening his mouth.

My throat clenched. This was it for me, now. Loneliness. No one wanted a handicapped kid for a friend. That thought made my blood feel like rivers of ice.

Which was not to say I could feel my blood at all.

* * *

"Rebecca called."

I remember the day my mom said this.

"She asked if she could come and visit."

It was a Tuesday, and I was about to get transferred.

See, I'd initially undergone treatment in a hospital. After that, it was on to a rehabilitation center. The hospital was north of Mount Radiance, eight hours from my home. The rehab center was closer to home, but only by about 50 miles or so.

I was still stranded in the middle of nowhere, pretty much.

And worse yet, there'd be no going home for me until I'd achieved an adequate degree of functionality. Bathroom stuff. Getting in and out of cars. Around corners. Even up and down stairs, if the occasion demanded it.

In the meantime, my parents would have to pass tests.

As if it wasn't bad enough that they were up here with me, racking up a massive hotel room bill...and as if it wasn't bad enough that they were watching their kid's life get twisted into a rare form of hell...

To top it all off, they had to be a pair of students, attending a class on how to manage the life of a paralyzed kid.

My mom muttered complaints about the nurses. She said she wasn't looking forward to the class, 'cause during the sign-up session – a little 15-minute meet and greet, in the downstairs hallway at the rehab center, which I'd still yet to see – they'd stared her up and down with cold eyes while throwing smiles and warmth at my father.

That wasn't the first time such a thing had happened. My dad, despite his troubles, was charming. He could make new friends in half a second, presuming he was sober enough to communicate with them. It wasn't that my mom wasn't social – just that when my dad was making the rounds, doing his charming thing, women lit up with immediate interest...

And immediately turned my mom into the enemy.

It would have been kind of funny if it didn't make my mom so mad.

Now, with their class about to start up, such drama was the last thing she needed. But of course she didn't want to waste too much breath complaining to me.

Which was part of why it gave her so much pleasure to say that word on that Tuesday:

"Rebecca."

* * *

It was the first time I'd felt real happiness since waking up.

For my parents, I'd been putting up a strong front. The way I saw it was, if I fell apart, they'd fall apart. I was at the center of this storm, and it therefore fell on me to try to hold that center together.

It wasn't something I wanted to do. Certainly wasn't something I'd ever planned on doing.

ROLLING HOME

But the alternative was clearly a world of chaos.

So despite the way I felt inside – not depressed, 'cause that wasn't the way my brain was made, but definitely confused and urgent – I reached for as much strength as possible in their presence.

The same went for my grandpa's presence, of course.

He'd only been there during my sedated stretch. I wish I could say I recall his presence. I do have memories of his voice, not far from my bed.

And other memories – worse ones – of that voice cracking.

Giving way to tears. Even sobs, maybe.

Eventually, it was decided amongst the grown-ups that he should wait for me back at home. Nobody was mad at him, least of all me, but he really didn't have a function up there at the time. It wasn't like he had to take any tests.

Nor was the guy my actual parent.

He was (accidentally) the source of this problem, but that didn't require him to be eternally vigilant at my side.

Though from what I gathered, from my parents' words, he wanted to be at my side forever...

That was Grandpa Angus for you. That was why I loved the guy.

But in light of the tragedy of his mistake, I kind of agreed that it was best for him to be at a distance for now. I'd have plenty of time to talk it through with him later.

And I didn't have a single bad word to say to the guy.

Maybe someone else would feel angry, but I saw the situation for what it was: The poor guy loved me with all his heart, and he'd made an awful mistake. Knowing this – seeing it with clarity – what would I gain from blowing up at him?

I had no doubt he was already torturing himself as it was.

Be that as it may, though I felt confident that my display of strength would be effective and convincing in my parents' presence, I wasn't at all sure about my grandpa. Maybe he'd be too sharp to buy it.

Maybe he'd see it as a facade, mounted for his benefit.

Yeah, I felt bad about it, but I was happier to not be seeing him right about now.

As for my friend, the girl, the source of my happiness...

I wanted to see Rebecca as soon as possible.

* * *

I hadn't had much communication with Rebecca before the accident.

She was somewhere between an acquaintance and a friend, but tilted a bit more in the acquaintance direction. We had the same lunch period, but none of the same classes. I got the sense she was one level above me academically, so our courses never intersected.

But I always liked seeing her at lunch.

Prior to the accident, before I was in for a long stretch of home-schooling, I sat with Double Mike and three other guys at lunch. Rebecca only sat with her friend Stacy, though. Just the two of them, across from each other, a few tables down from the one I shared with Mike.

Once in a while, Stacy would be absent and Rebecca would be alone (or vice versa). On one of those occasions, I got brave and pulled up the empty seat across from Rebecca's.

She seemed startled for a second, as though I was gonna be difficult or play a prank on her or something. I remember her hands went to each side of her tray, which to me was an indicator that she was thinking of getting up and leaving.

Double Mike and the rest of my crew saw what I was doing. They were looking, but when I glanced their way they all looked elsewhere.

I looked back at Rebecca.

Smiled at her.

"You're all alone," I said.

"Yeah." She was blushing. "My friend Stacy has the flu."

"Ouch," I said. "That'll last for a while. I had it last year and it went on for like 10 days."

"Yeah," she repeated. "I hope she comes back

soon."

I could sense she was uptight. Trying not to say the wrong thing. As for me, I didn't exactly know what I was doing. I had ordered a cheeseburger, but only hamburgers had been available. So the cooks had told me to wait 10 minutes while they got the cheese from the freezer and put some new patties on the burner.

So, having seen Rebecca there all by herself, I figured there was no harm in spending those minutes with her.

Only now 10 minutes was starting to seem like 1,000. I didn't have Double Mike to back me up. And clearly she was kind of shy, which was no good since I was kind of shy, too.

So much for my dim hope that she'd end up carrying the conversation...

I looked at her. She looked back. We both smiled. It was dreadfully clear that if our silence went on for even a few more moments, we'd officially have entered awkward territory. So I had to dig in. Had to think fast.

Had to not let this go down as a ridiculous moment.

"Can I sit here with you?" I asked. "Until Stacy comes back?"

Her lips started moving, but they weren't making any words...

"I mean," I said, knowing that neither of us could handle a prolonged encounter, "just for the beginning of each period. You know: so you have company."

Still: her lips kept going. No words yet, however...

I cocked my thumb at Double Mike and the boys. "I'd invite you to come with us," I went on. "But those guys are pigs. You'd have a terrible time."

Now she laughed.

Good: that was better than her silence.

"You can totally sit here with me," she said.

Her face was really, really red. Had she seen herself in a mirror right then, she probably would have been mortified. I certainly wasn't about to tell her what was going on. Hell, my own face was feeling a little warm, too. God only knows what I looked like at that moment.

"I'm T—" I began, stretching out my hand.

"Tucker," she interjected. She knew.

"And you're Rebecca."

We shook hands. She nodded.

It was the last time I ever touched her before the hospital.

* * *

I didn't know what I was doing.

Part of me just wanted to look cool in front of Mike and company. But the deeper part of me really wanted to get to know Rebecca. Turned out Stacy was only gone for six days, diced up by a weekend. I spent the first 10 minutes of lunch with Rebecca on each one of those days. We talked about how many siblings we had. Talked about what our favorite movies were. Talked about which teachers we liked and which ones we hated.

I wanted to ask at a couple points if she was planning on going to a couple different parties, but I knew that wasn't what this girl was all about. She definitely had more than one friend – I was aware of at least three other girls, in addition to Stacy – but just the same she wasn't known for being very social.

Which was surprising, since Rebecca was really pretty.

I mean: *really* pretty.

She was easily in the top five best-looking girls in the junior class, if not the top three. What I liked about her most was that she didn't wear a lot of makeup. She had natural beauty, whether she knew it or not.

As I sat across from her on those six days, I really wanted to find a way to tell her that. But somehow an opening never came. And I didn't want to seem weird or overeager. So little by little, we established something more along the lines of a friendship than a flirtation, much less a romance.

And to be honest, it wasn't even that much of a friendship.

I, for one, was going through so much at the time. I felt like a giant clock was ticking its way toward college, and that before I knew it I'd wake up in a whole new world, with no clue as to what would happen next. It made me nervous. Sometimes I opened up about my feelings to Mike, or even to my mom. But the truth was, I could have used someone to bond with on that point. Not even to talk about the future, just to talk openly – truthfully – in general.

I looked at Rebecca from across that lunch table and I so wanted her to be that person.

But the lame part was that I didn't have the emotional vocabulary to take things there. Nor did I feel confident that she'd even follow if I led the way. She was nice and everything, but she never shook off that nervous vibe completely. Each time I sat with her felt like the first time. It didn't deepen or get natural; it always stayed a little stiff and formal.

Until, on the sixth day, when we had something resembling a "moment" between us.

"Hey." I sat down. I had my tray with me already; most of the time my order was available right away.

"Hey," she said. "Stacy's better. She's coming back tomorrow."

I nodded. I felt my emotions slipping toward something like hurt, as I didn't know why she'd volunteer that info. Was that relief I detected underneath her voice? Or maybe she was just being informational. She struck me as that kind of person. She just wanted me to know so there'd be no surprises.

I skipped being sensitive and went with that interpretation.

"Oh yeah?" I asked. "Better, huh?"
She nodded.

I looked around. Double Mike was watching me, but as always, once I looked he looked away. That punk had never even asked me about Rebecca. Never even made so much as a joke about it when I walked back to our table. He just acted like my thing with her was business as usual.

Maybe Mike had never been such a good friend, after all.

I looked back at Rebecca. "You know," I said, "you should come with us sometime. To a party. Would you be into that?"

"Oh..." Her eyes were far away.

I instantly had no doubt that she wouldn't be into that at all.

In fact, part of me wondered whether she took my words as an invitation to go on a date. But no – she couldn't really take it that way, could she? I mean, it was a *party.* And there wasn't even a specific one I had in mind. It seemed like lately, every weekend or so, somebody's parents were either going away or willing to be cool enough to stay upstairs. So I knew something was bound to materialize, and I figured that with 30 other people around she wouldn't see it as anything resembling a date.

She finally gave her gaze back to me. She said, "It's just...my parents, you know."

Ah. I was starting to understand her a little more...Suddenly it all made sense: the stiffness, the (let's face it) awkwardness. Maybe her parents weren't too keen on letting her hang around boys.

"Say no more." I waved my hand. "I understand."

"Plus, I have to study for the SATs..."

"Ah, yeah." I resisted making mention of the fact that they weren't coming up for over six more months. I was planning on studying for them, too, but really didn't expect to dig in until after Thanksgiving.

"I totally get you."

And I totally did. Just the same, though, it was rejection. And I'm only human. So it hurt a little bit. The very hurt that I'd managed to push back against when she'd told me about Stacy was now rearing its ugly head in a whole new form.

Damn it. Why'd I have to be so sensitive?

Anyway, I figured I had to do something here. I was officially about six minutes away from losing my daily routine with Rebecca. In the meantime, I really didn't want to walk around for the rest of the week (or for the rest of my life – who could know?) feeling bad about getting turned down.

So I said to her, "It'd be nice to hang out again. Or, for the first time..."

I smiled. She laughed.

"You know," I went on, "outside of school."

There it was again: that redness. It didn't even bother to stop at pink: her cheeks went right for an aggressive, ketchup-flavored, newborn-styled red.

I liked it.

I loved her.

Or maybe I was just out of my mind.

In any case, she gave me a nod. She said, "Yeah, that'd be great."

And that right there was our little moment.

But I didn't have the guts to try to follow up on it. I mean, I'd already expended a surprising dose of bravery just by hopping into that empty seat.

However, little did I know that as fate would have it, Rebecca would be the one to follow up with *me*. Little did I know that the moment when those germs entered Stacy's system, spreading a sickness about her body and making her trade school for bed, my own life story was being reconstructed in such a way as to have a whole new character in it.

And little did I know that the moment when Grandpa Angus made that fateful error in regard to not packing his holster, he was effectively bridging the gap between me and Rebecca for the second time...

For the first time, when we were strangers, I had bridged it.

But the second time, it would be all her.

* * *

"Rebecca *White*?"

I was giving my mother the third degree.

"I don't know. She didn't say her last name."

Everything in me wanted to sit up in bed, but that process was something that I was far from having mastered. Regardless, my *attention level* had perked up – about as far as it could go.

"You have to know. Was she from my school?"

"Well, she was your age, Tucker."

"How do you know?"

"Because I have ears."

My mom smiled. She had a gift for sarcasm. It ran in the family, in fact. But at this moment, I wasn't really in the mood for anything less than utter, blinding clarity.

Yes, I knew full well that it was "my" Rebecca. My buddy. My lunch-mate. The one I made blush. But mind you, I'd fallen into one hell of an ugly predicament here. Life had very recently issued me a stark education on how unpredictable and insane it could be.

So when my mom started mentioning "Rebecca", I got a little paranoid. I had to make absolutely certain that it was the right one.

My mom understood this – every speck of it. She knew that I knew who the girl was, but she also knew that I was just making extra sure. That was my mom: She just knew things like that. So she gave it some thought and said the right words, the very words I needed to hear in order to claim some calmness:

"Since she's willing to drive seven hours to come and see you, I get the feeling she kind of likes you, Tucker..."

My mom smirked at me. Gave me a little wink, even. Or maybe I just imagined the wink. In any case, there was a knowing sparkle in her eye. It told me not only that, yes, Rebecca dug me, but also that, yes, my mom knew full well she had just said exactly the right thing.

And I couldn't help but smile.

It hurt to smile, actually. I hadn't given my cheek muscles much of a workout in that hospital. In fact, I can't recall having had a reason to smile previous to hearing my mother say the R-word.

* * *

But right away, there were problems.

Almost five seconds after I felt my whole being light up with joy, I descended into the depths of sheer naked self-consciousness:

Would she still like me?

Did she just pity me?

Would she be more awkward than ever now?

Oh, no. Maybe this wasn't such good news after all. Maybe I was better off avoiding this encounter.

No, I couldn't do that. I had to make the most of it. It was literally the only good thing happening for me at that moment, shy of the fact that that bullet hadn't ended my life. I couldn't allow myself to be the guy who sabotaged something good just because I'd been surrounded by so much bad.

I had to let it be what it was:

It was good that she'd called.

ROLLING HOME

It was good that she'd thought of me.

And it was absolutely good that she was coming.

* * *

"Can you brush my hair?"

I was speaking to Nancy now. Nancy was the nurse who came in daily to rinse and lubricate my wound. I liked her; we had a good rapport. She was always in an upbeat mood. The first time I saw her, this annoyed me, 'cause I thought it was just a show she put on to make the sick and handicapped folks feel better.

However, in time, I came to see that it was probably just her nature.

In fact, that's probably how she got the job.

And being around her made me feel good. Almost as thought her vibes were coming into my own body. I remembered reading somewhere that all of us are vibrational creatures, and that the energy we send out travels eternally, without ever stopping or slowing down, so we had best make an effort to emit the best vibration we could.

Nancy was a master at this.

"Why you want me to brush your hair?" she asked. "You got a hot date?"

I smiled. Already, she was touching my hair, as though checking it out, the better to ascertain how she might indeed comb it if she ended up doing so.

"Something like that," I said.

"Mmm hmm." She let my bangs plop down. It occurred to me that I was probably overdue for a cut, but given the nature of my circumstances, a comb would do just fine. "Well, you're transferring tomorrow, so if I comb it now, somebody else'll have to next time."

"That's fine," I said. "I just want it nice and neat."

I wanted, in other words, to start feeling a little better about my appearance.

So first she went and got the moisturizer, and went to work on my wound. It always felt like my neck was six times the size of a normal human neck when she massaged it. Her fingers felt like they were disappearing down into a slimy, gnarly, inflamed mass of bone and tissue.

Which they were.

After she lubed and toned the wound, I became aware of a black comb in her hand. I would've preferred to see a brush, given how knotted and funky my hair felt at the time, but hey, beggars can't be choosers.

She went to work. Took her time. Got into those knots. After it was over, she held up a mirror before my face.

Not bad. She'd actually slicked it back nice and tight. I'd been expecting more of a general neatening, but Nancy had managed to get in there deep. I smiled at my own reflection.

I approved.

Now Rebecca had to...

ROLLING HOME

* * *

The rehab center was called The Colsen Institute. From the first time I heard those words, I kind of thought they made it sound like a military institution.

As it turned out, that wasn't far from the case.

It wasn't that the staff was all that demanding (even though my mom kept issuing pretty grim reports about her nurse instructors), it was that the whole place felt like gloom and doom. No matter what they did – play music, crack the curtains – I couldn't shake this general feeling of crushing sadness.

At first I thought it was just me, but in time I came to find that I was actually one of the happier patients...

Other patients were known to scream and shout, to the point of actually throwing tantrums, like three-year-olds. In fact, not a day went by when there wasn't some altercation or another. Everybody around me was always complaining: patients complaining about staff members, staff members complaining (under their breath) about patients, visitors complaining about both.

Naturally, I hadn't gone in expecting a rehab center for newly disabled patients to be overflowing with good cheer, but it turned out I'd had it pretty good back at the hospital. Those guys back there knew how to throw on the charm. Here, it was more like a general understanding that everything was already miserable to begin with, so there was no point in working against it.

That started to get to me. I started to press my parents about how soon I'd be able to go home. Moreover, I started to press them about those phone calls from Rebecca. By now, they were in the process of scheduling her visit. Two weeks into my stay at Colsen, there had already been a total of three phone calls between her and my mom.

And Rebecca's big visit was one Friday away – eight days in the future, to be exact.

I kept confirming with my mom that it was on. I couldn't believe Rebecca was making the drive. My mom said she was bringing Stacy with her, but that Stacy would stay back at their hotel room. Since there was a hotel room in the picture, I figured Rebecca's parents were paying for it. And that meant Stacy's parents were possibly chipping in, too. At the very least, the factors of the long drive, the best friend coming, and the overnight hotel stay were making this into a very big deal.

The more details I learned, the more I fantasized that this was as big a deal for Rebecca as it was for me. Even though by any rational measurement I knew that couldn't be true, I still clung to the fantasy. Maybe she loved me. Maybe she regretted not partying with me.

Those thoughts were pretty much all I had to maintain a shred of sanity.

* * *

ROLLING HOME

My dad, meanwhile, had his own ways of coping.

One day, during a break from him and my mom's class, he popped into my room for a visit. I shared the room with Mortimer, an old guy who'd just had a leg removed, but Morty was in physical therapy for an hour.

Right away, upon my dad's entrance, I knew something was wrong.

And in a place like Colsen, where everything seems wrong every second, that's saying a lot.

The "wrong" with my dad wasn't a gloomy wrong, though. It was the way he smelled. The way he was walking. The fact that he seemed overjoyed to see me, when we'd just spent time together after breakfast.

What the hell?

Was the guy actually *drinking?*

My heart started beating fast. I couldn't feel it in my torso, but I could feel the warmth of the blood rushing to my face. First, my pulse rose 'cause of fear: my initial instinct was to get worried about him being kicked out of his class.

Maybe he'd never even be able to take me home!

That particular thought is what turned fear into anger. Why was he doing this to me? God, I understood the guy was devastated, but did he really have to go and risk my entire future?

I mean, did he have to be so irresponsible?

He made his way to the window. Looked out at the sunny afternoon, which Colsen had a wonderful way of making seem grim and apocalyptic.

"Beautiful day today, huh?" he asked me.

This wasn't him trying to have a good attitude for my sake.

This was him drunk out of his mind and seeing beauty where there wasn't any.

Sure, he held it together okay. You wouldn't know he'd been drinking if you didn't know him well. But I could *feel* it in him: the ease of his movements. The sudden fluid quality of his muscles. The improbable lightness of his attitude.

"Dad..."

Still, his eyes were aimed out the window.

I kind of think that based on my tone, he could intuit that I was about to say something tense. Which, of course, I was...

He didn't say anything. Kept looking out. Was probably trying to find a clean, solid thought to hang onto.

"Dad..."

Finally: there they were.

His eyes.

"What's up, kid?"

"You can't do this..."

I felt so nervous, saying these words. Never once had I called the man out about his drinking. Never once had I ventured into a discussion remotely that serious, unless you count my words from back of my grandpa's car:

"Tell Mom and Dad I love them."

Which was true.

I did love them. And I wasn't about to let my dad get lost here.

"You can't be drinking in here."

There: I'd said it.

"They'll find out and..."

"Lower your voice, lower your voice." His eyes were aimed downward. Fingers were then raised, pinching the bridge of his nose.

He left the room.

Somehow, though, I didn't feel as though the conversation had been cut short. On the contrary, I felt I'd said exactly what I'd needed to say.

And more importantly, the guy had heard me.

It was a step.

* * *

"I want to work my arms," I said.

I was talking to Tony. "Big Tony", they called him. Note that I said, "they", 'cause I never called him "Big." To me, the guy was just Tony.

And to be honest, he was lucky I called him anything at all...

Tony was technically part of the nursing staff, but since his skill-set pertained entirely to recuperating disabled people, he didn't have the personality of a regular nurse. He was more like a coach, or a drill sergeant, even. From the first moment I met him, I didn't like him. He seemed to walk around in a cage constructed of his own superiority complex. The message I got from him (without him saying a word) was "I know you're paralyzed, and I don't care. I'm not impressed. So I'm gonna treat you just like I treat anyone else.

"In fact, just to prove my point, I'll treat you worse."

Tony, like the other half dozen members of the recuperation team, had something of a shady past. Judging from all the tattoos snaking up and down his muscular arms, it seemed like he had been in prison, even though he never mentioned anything like that. Or maybe he'd been in gangs, and gotten out.

Anyway, he had an air of the "street" around him. In and of itself, that was no problem, but the thing about Tony was, he wasn't even street smart. He seemed to have no common sense. To be honest, he was just a jerk.

"Why you so obsessed with your arms?" he asked me.

"I'm not obsessed. They're the part of me that works the best."

"What about your head? Your mind?"

"You know what I mean."

"Kid: I'm afraid I don't."

He leaned in pretty close to me when he said those last words. I could smell the tuna fish he'd had for lunch, not only on his breath but in the whiskers of his unshaven face. I inhaled and exhaled.

We were perched atop a little stretch of sloping sidewalk, maybe 20 yards across, that Tony always made a point to use while we went out practicing the wheelchair. For some reason – "standard hospital procedure," I was told – they only provided the patients with power wheelchairs, as opposed to manual ones.

For me, this was a major problem.

On the face of it, it would seem that power chairs were preferable, since they're motorized and require less effort on the part of the person in the chair. This, however, wasn't adequate in my case; I actually wanted to *use* my chair, not just be a passenger in it. Reason being, as I tried to explain to Tony, my arms were the best remaining part of my body (save for my head, of course, but in terms of mobility, my arms had a *clear* advantage), so I wanted them to be as buff, capable, and even powerful as humanly possible.

His inability to understand that was driving me crazy.

"Go down this hill," he said.

"Not a hill," I muttered.

"What's that you say?"

He actually cupped a hand around the back of his ear, resembling Hulk Hogan when he wanted the fans to scream louder. Only Tony – as far as I could surmise – had no fans whatsoever.

And he certainly couldn't count me among them.

"Not – a – hill," I repeated.

I was right, and he knew it. At best, it was a kind of ramp. Even the official wheelchair ramp out in front of the facility made for a steeper climb.

I knew I was in trouble, then. For suddenly I couldn't see any sunshine coming from the sky. The reason? Tony was now hovering over me like my own personal storm cloud.

"Attitude is everything in life," he said.

"I know," I replied. I mean, he only said that like 19 times an hour.

"So if you have a bad attitude, where's that gonna get you?"

"If I don't have a manual wheelchair, where's THAT gonna get me?"

His eyebrows sprung up. He was newly acknowledging the fact that, yes, we were having ourselves a little altercation here.

"Do I write up the budget? Do I make the decisions?"

"No." I made no eye contact with him.

"So how in the world could I get you a manual chair?"

"I don't know," I snapped. I looked at him, my eyes catching the only piece of sun that his body wasn't blocking out. "Be assertive. Have the right *attitude*."

We made long eye contact. He didn't like that very much. He brushed his nose with his fingertips, then – as though abandoning a lost cause – left my sight.

For a moment I didn't know where Tony was. I sat there kind of hoping that he'd walked away, maybe to teach me some dumb lesson or to prove some ridiculous point. And maybe his refusal to have hung in there with me would even end up getting him fired.

A kid can dream, can't he?

About a minute and a half went by. For the first part of it, I heard Tony behind me, walking away. Then there was no sound, save for that of my own breath. I thought to turn the chair around and check on where he was, but I didn't want him thinking I cared.

When Tony returned, he was a little out of breath, for he'd known that leaving me alone was against the rules, and that rushing was the optimum course of action.

More importantly, dangling from the fingertips of each of his hands was a bright orange cone, the kind you see in the street to mark detours and/or areas you're not supposed to cross.

"What's this?" My tone was flat, borderline menacing.

"This is today's test of will. Today's test of attitude."

Tony marched down to the bottom of the slope. He then set the cones shy of three feet apart from each other. After he did so, he stepped back from them and crossed his arms over his chest.

Then he looked at me.

And I looked at him.

"What's this?" I asked again, this time with an audible tinge of irritation.

"Go through them," he said, in the calculated tone of a super villain who knows he's requesting something impossible.

"What?" The word came out all whiny, like I wasn't his patient but his teenage son.

"You can do it," he said.

Oh, yeah, sure. Now Tony was suddenly a motivational speaker!

"They're too close together," I said.

"Nuh uh."

"Uh huh."

He smiled. And yeah, I'll admit it was a little funny, in a cheesy sitcom kind of way. Aiming my chin at the cones, I said, "How's this gonna help with my arms?"

"It won't. Like I said: It'll help your will and your attitude."

"My will is fine."

"Then how 'bout the 'tude?"

I almost cracked up laughing. Not with him – *at* him. Did he actually just stand there and say the word "'tude" with a straight face?

My reality had somehow turned completely ridiculous.

"I don't see how squeezing between those cones will help my attitude."

"It takes a good attitude to make it happen. So try,

Tucker. We don't have all day."

He checked his watch, but I don't think he even read the time. He was just putting on a show, like all the other recuperation staff members. Their job was just a power trip. Bark orders, play the coach, push people past their limits. Inspirational in theory, but depressing in reality. Apparently wherever they'd come from, they didn't have very much in the way of authority or power. At least not in an authentic sense; at home, they probably had to force people to respect them. Here, however, it was a different story. They wore fancy licenses around their necks, tucked into shiny laminated holders. "Tony Crawford."

I couldn't *stand* this guy.

I eyed the cones. The only reason I did so was that, believe it or not, it was preferable to continuing my conversation with him. Studying them, I gave myself 70/30 odds of making it through, in favor of not making it. I was actually curious to test it out, if only to see how accurate my guess was.

I suppose that's what happens when you're bored out of your mind.

"Okay," I said, "I'll do this. But only under one condition."

"Go."

"You'll ask your bosses to get a manual chair. I mean: How expensive can it be?"

"Kid: They have plenty of manual chairs back there. But they don't supply them to our unit. Way it's always been, way it'll always be. Now come on: Move it."

My blood began to boil. This guy was some smug piece of work. Here he was, actually admitting that the solution, a manual chair, was well within our reach, yet refusing to do anything about because he didn't want to upset the established order of things.

So I let it go. I just activated my chair. And it flew forward, like a stone from a catapult, rolling down the slope toward those two cones.

As it turned out, my prediction had been right.

No way I could possibly make it through. Tony had probably known that, too. So at the last possible second, I swerved and angled my chair sideways against the cones.

They both knocked over. One rolled a couple feet away.

Tony looked down at me. I looked up at him.

"Gee," I said, "I'm not sure I feel my attitude's changed."

Tony just frowned and shook his head.

* * *

The next day was a Tuesday, which meant Tony was off. In his place was Alba, a woman who looked polite and meek from the outside but was actually possessed of a pretty sour disposition.

Almost as though she were overcompensating for

seeming too polite and meek...

I didn't care, though. She didn't intimidate me. Come to think of it, not much of anything that had once intimidated me was very frightening anymore. Who cared about these people and their lousy attitudes (as they spouted endless "wisdom" about the need to have a good attitude)? I was here for one reason and one reason only:

To learn.

So regardless of how their personalities were structured, I was going to take value with me from this environment. Looking up at Alba, I whispered, "I saw some manual chairs in the cafeteria."

"So?" She actually shrugged at me, shoulders hanging high for half a second.

"So can we grab one?"

"Not supposed to."

"I know. But why?"

Again with the shrugging. She said, "You have to learn the power chair. How to maneuver."

Well, that statement was certainly consistent with our daily outings all around the grounds. All we did was *maneuver*: turn corners, move forward, move backward, take tricky turns, retrace our steps.

And I'd figured out every last bit of it in about two seconds.

In fact, the entire staff seemed to know that. They wouldn't admit it – they weren't about to cheer me on – but the evidence was right there in front of them. I wasn't like the old ladies around us who'd broken their hips in the shower; I was a kid; I had youth in me. Fast reflexes, a nimble mind.

Stuff that I wasn't intent upon letting go to waste.

Gathering my breath, I asked Alba, "Will you really get in trouble if you get me one? Just blame it on me. Say I mastered the power chair."

I smiled. It seemed as though she thought of smiling back, but changed her mind at the last second.

"You ain't no master, son."

"Come on: every day, it's the same drills. I'm bored. I want to build up my arms."

She, like Tony – and like all their colleagues – had heard this plenty of times before. And like all the rest of them, she remained unmoved. The situation just kept getting more insane. It's not like I wanted special treatment just because of the position I was in...but then again, in light of that position, would it really be the worst thing in the world to just do me a favor?

"I can't leave you alone out here," she said, giving me a frown.

That was it: Beautiful! A milestone moment. For her statement actually showed that she was *thinking* of doing me the favor. At least on some level, or at least in part. For rather than just shutting me down altogether, she was stating a practical reason for refusing, complete with issuing me what seemed to be a true frown of sympathy.

Good. I'll take it. Better than nothing.

In my position, I found out fast, you take what you can get...

"I'll go with you," I said.

"To the cafeteria?" Her eyes were popping out. It was, in fact, the most colorful expression I'd yet seen on Alba's face.

"Yeah. Why not?"

"Everybody's in there."

"Come on," I said. I spun my chair toward the building's front. "We'll be in and out in two seconds."

Well maybe not that fast, but fast enough. Who would notice? Everybody would be too busy eating. The manual chairs were lined up along the wall nearest to the door, the same way you see shopping carts lined up outside of grocery stores. Unused. Unwanted.

Not likely to be missed.

"Wait," she said, following me toward the building's front ramp, "hold up."

She stepped right in front of me. Risky move, that, since I could've very easily run her over, what with me being such a "non-master" on the power chair. "Where I come from, things don't go this way."

"Where do you come from?" I asked her, not entirely interested, but buying a little time.

"San Diego," she said, and right away I knew that she'd come from Mexico, and crossed the border into San Diego. Or her parents had before she was born. Either way, her native language was Spanish; that much had been clear from our very first session. And Alba didn't seem like the type of woman who'd grown up with a swimming pool and a swing-set in her backyard. No, she was tough. Like the rest of her unit.

Exuding "street."

"So how do things work in San Diego?" I asked, picturing all my parents' friends from that area – the lawyers, the doctors, the plastic surgeons – and not voicing the irony screaming from beneath these images.

"I do you a favor, you do me a favor," she said.

In typical Alba fashion, she was speaking flatly, betraying not a speck of emotion, to the point where it was almost surreal hearing her say these words. Just the same, at least getting the manual chair wasn't off the table.

"Okaaay," I said. "What favor can I do you?"

My pulse quickened a bit, as I really had no clue what she could possibly ask for.

"You put in a good report," she said. "Say I'm your favorite aid."

"Okay, yeah, of course," I said, suddenly relieved.

"You promise?"

"Promise." I gave her my most confidence-inducing smile.

"And it's true," I said. "You are my favorite."

"Oh," Alba said – as she actually blushed! – "you are such a liar."

I laughed. "Maybe," I said. "But you'll definitely be my favorite after today."

That was the moment for me and Alba. From that point on, we had a bond. And apparently taking the manual chair wasn't any kind of big deal after all, 'cause if it was she wouldn't have requested a report from me. For the existence of the report would draw attention to the two of us, but that didn't seem to bother her in any way.

In fact, when we entered the cafeteria, Alba looked at one of the administrators as she grabbed a manual chair and said, "Gonna borrow this. He's too advanced for the power chair."

The administrator, seeming bored beyond belief, just let out half a yawn and said, "Okay."

Then he left the cafeteria and didn't look back, apparently en route to his office to fall asleep for three hours...

As I followed Alba back out toward the courtyard, all I could think about was what a jerk that Tony was. All along, he could've worked the same deal, but he chose not to for reasons that he alone knew. Was he afraid of his superiors? Did he truly wish to test my will and attitude?

Nah, I think that guy was just hateful.

As for Alba, on the other hand: She was proving to be really cool.

* * *

It took us a few minutes to get me from one chair to the other. We didn't have the benefit of a bed – meaning a higher surface – to grant some natural momentum to the process. So Alba bear-hugged me and lifted me out of one chair, then sloppily and diagonally positioned me in the other.

At first, I got a terrible feeling. I instantly thought the manual chair was a bad idea. It felt so rickety and old. And my body was bigger in proportion to it than to the power chair. Meanwhile, the power chair was simply more comfortable. Modern. Cushioned. Its vibe was stronger, despite how much I disliked its function.

I looked at Alba. I felt kind of helpless, like a little kid being expected to ride his bike for the first time minus training wheels. Maybe I was underrating the manual chair out of nerves. Maybe I'd wanted it so bad that I was now guarding myself against being let down.

A flicker of Rebecca fired across my mind.

I then positioned my hands atop each wheel. I thought of my grandfather – the legendary Angus. He for one wouldn't give way to fear. No, he'd see this thing all the way through.

Wouldn't he love to know I was thinking that? That I was drawing inspiration from the very man who'd caused me so much grief?

That was Grandpa Angus for you; impossible to hate.

My hands felt sloppy on the tires; I couldn't achieve a decent grip. The thought of rolling this thing forward wasn't exactly daunting, but a little intimidating just the same.

"Go for it," Alba said, her hair and face catching the midday light. "You can do it."

She wasn't being corny, either. She really meant it. I liked her. She'd get a good report.

I gave her a tiny nod and proceeded to PUSH!

* * *

It was wild. Amazing, actually.

My arms felt like brand new body parts, newly attached to me via God himself. I'd never known them in this way before. Never felt so free, nor strong.

Most of that, of course, stemmed from my happiness.

I could *move* again! Meaning I was in control. I wasn't subject to the electronic will of a motor; I was actually speaking to my arms through my brain, and dancing with them, letting them guide my chair.

It was awe-inspiring. Hope-inducing. It kicked the wind right through my hair.

My hands remained a pain in the butt, though. They weren't always on sound speaking terms with what my arms and wrists wanted to do. Something deep in my brain kept trying to fire into my hands, to make them more nimble and complex in their motions, but they remained as they were: stiff and bent, a pair of flesh-and-bone hooks.

But I thanked God for the use of my arms. I didn't

just thank him in a direct sense, for having spared them in the accident, but in the sense that God had designed my body in such a way as to let the nerves controlling my arms be preserved when so much else of me went south.

Alba tried to keep up behind me. On my own, I could go faster than I could with the motor. Maybe that fact had been behind their regulations all along. In any case, this was the first time since the accident when I really felt excited and inspired. Sure, Rebecca's pending visit was a source of positive energy, but that was still pending.

This was actually happening.

Before long, I felt the muscles in my arms start to tense. I'd clearly worked them too hard right out the gate. They weren't in pain or anything, but just the feeling of tension made me slow down and call it a day. After all, the last thing I needed was to mess with the most active part of my body.

As Alba rolled me back toward the front, I thanked her for the "opportunity." I felt a little silly using that word – like I was walking out of a job interview or something – but somehow I couldn't find an adequate substitute.

She'd given me a chance to live. A shot of freedom.

"You're welcome," she said, as we entered the door, and thus all the darkness beyond it.

"Can we do it again tomorrow?"

"Tomorrow's Tony," she said.

ROLLING HOME

I sighed. "Can we do it next time you're here?"

She laughed as we moved toward the elevators. "Of course," she said, and the two of us shared a little laugh.

* * *

The next time I saw Tony, things got a little ugly.

By then, he knew all about Alba and my little habit of sneaking manual chairs from the cafeteria. In fact, it was no secret; tons of people saw us working with the manual ones. In the end, nobody seemed to care. What were they gonna do, beat up on a poor kid about his selection of wheelchairs?

But for reasons known only to him, Tony was grumpy about the whole thing. He never got specific as to exactly why. In my opinion, I just don't think he liked seeing me get my way. Almost as though he just didn't like another person being happy.

Which was ridiculous, seeing as how limited my chances at happiness had become.

"What's your problem?" I asked him.

The words came out suddenly. We were practicing curves in the motor chair right beside a small lake at the edge of the Colsen grounds. The lake had some ducks in it, and a machine alongside of it where you could get some duck food for a quarter. Most of the people around us were senior citizens. Tony decided to start taking me there 'cause he knew that if I didn't get my curves right, I had somewhat of a risk of tipping over into the water.

I say "somewhat" because it wasn't a real risk. We were too many feet away from the water – about five or six, I guessed – for that to ever happen. And besides, even Tony, as much of a sad sack as he was, was too careful to take that kind of risk.

So it wasn't the presence of the water that got to me. It was the stupid grass. The chair just couldn't handle very well on the grass. In the manual chair, I had a better time off of hard surfaces, but in general, wheelchairs and grass just didn't mix. Everyone knew that. Why didn't he?

As I struggled, knowing that we had no reason whatsoever to be using this chair and not the manual one – and knowing full well that every moment I spent in that motor chair, my arms were just getting softer – I finally spat the "What's your problem?" at him.

He didn't like that very much.

Ever the coach, he made a "time-out" symbol with his hands: a great big T-bone hovering over me. "Hold up!" he barked.

I stopped rolling forward.

His chest thrust outward and inward as he breathed. I'm pretty sure that was actual rage inside his eyes. Looking down at me, he said, "Want to know my problem?"

"Yeah!" I wasn't kidding around now, either.

"YOU!"

ROLLING HOME

He said it loud enough for some of the seniors to turn and look. But I didn't care what they thought. Looking over at a man in perfect physical health yelling at a kid who couldn't walk, whose side were they actually gonna take?

"WHY?" I asked him. "I do everything you tell me to!"

"I told you not to use the manual chair."

"How come??"

"Because it's against the rules!"

"But nobody cares about the stupid rules!"

I could feel the redness in my face. Pure heat. RAGE heat. Were I able to punch him, I probably would have.

He wiped his nose with his hand: his classic "getting down to business" gesture. He then circled behind me, stomped a lever on the rear of the chair, and proceeded to push me away from the lake.

"Where we going?" I asked him, after several deadly seconds of silence.

"You'll see."

"Tell me!"

I could hear him breathing. It was mad dog breath. He, like me, was ready for blood. "Want you to meet someone," he said.

And the next thing I knew, he was rolling me beyond the gates of Colsen.

* * *

Two blocks away from The Colsen Institute was a convenience store. As Tony guided me toward its front door, I briefly entertained the comical possibility of him buying me some soda and potato chips and then apologizing.

But maybe I shouldn't have been laughing inside. Maybe this dude was actually trying to kidnap me!

That thought didn't cross my mind until we curved toward the alleyway beside the store. Wouldn't that be ironic, for Tony the big rule-follower to actually commit a crime?

Fortunately, he did no such thing. Instead, he introduced me to a man named James.

James was homeless. He stank pretty bad, actually. God only knew how long he'd been living on the street, but from the looks of him I'd estimate most of his life.

His *long* life. He had white hair. He was at least 70.

But I didn't get to know him all that well. Instead, I mostly listened as Tony whipped up a little conversation with him:

"How you doin', James?"

"Can't complain."

"Can't complain, huh? Fall weather, gets pretty cold at night. Must be hard."

"Ah, I don't drink, it's haaard. I take a drink..."

"Yeah, I gotcha. Liquor keeps you warm at night, huh?"

"That'd be 'bout right."

"Say, James..." There Tony went wiping his nose

again. "...I'm curious: How's business?"

James's expression, hazy as it was, changed a drop. Like he was an animal on the defensive, ready to be pounced. "Don't talk business to me. What-are-you-a-cop??"

Tony laughed. "Nah, got plenty of friends who're cops, though. We didn't start out that way."

Tony looked right into my eyes when he said his next words:

"We started out as enemies. When they arrested me."

My throat buckled a little. Tony had never been so open about his past. Looking back at James, he said, "Why don't you tell my friend Tucker here what you do?"

James looked at me. I wanted to disappear. "Why? He buyin'?"

"Buyin'?" asked Tony. "I don't know. You shoot heroin, Tucker?"

My mouth was real dry at that moment – so much so that when I said, "No," my lips made a clicking sound as they came apart.

"I didn't think so. Just the same, James: Why don't you come with us to Colsen? Tell Tucker more about what you do?"

"What are you doing?" I asked Tony.

He shushed me. Looking back at James, he said, "How's that sound? You follow us there?"

"Go to hell!"

"To hell? Why's that?"

Seeming ashamed, Tony let his gaze drift else-where.

What Tony said next shocked me to my core: "See, James here's like you, Tucker, only luckier. 'Cause when he got shot, he kept his hands, his torso, his neck, and even his hips.

"The only thing James lost was the use of his legs."

"But they stole my chair!" James yelled out. I could swear I saw teardrops forming atop his eyes.

"Hear that?" Tony asked me. "Stole his chair. Shame, huh?"

I had no clue where this game was going, but I liked Tony then less than ever. "Why don't we get him a new one, then?" I sneered at Tony.

Tony smiled. "Now that'd be nice, wouldn't it? Brand new chair. Only problem is, chairs cost money. And James don't have two pennies to scrape together."

James, whose eyes were now clearly dripping, simply turned his head and looked away.

* * *

Tony let me think about what I'd seen as he wheeled me back. Didn't say a word, just breathed and grunted.

I tried to form the point inside my head. Whatever it was escaped me, though. Was that a warning of some kind? That if I didn't improve my attitude, I'd start us-ing dope? The whole thing made no sense.

'Til Tony clarified it.

We were positioned at the bottom of the main ramp out front. Looking at me, Tony seemed far more calm than he had back at the lake. When he made his point, it sneaked up on me. In retrospect, I kind of wished I'd figured it out on my own:

"I broke rules, kid," he said. "Growing up. Every damn rule you can imagine. I stole, I used drugs, I was cruel to women. But prison knocked all that stuff out of me, even though you still look at me like I ain't legit."

I breathed. "I look at you like that 'cause you're too hard on me."

"Well if I am," he said, "then there's a reason. See, I broke rules and I got out. I was saved. James broke rules and look at him."

"But I'm not James. I have a comfortable family. I have people in my life..."

"Tucker..." I could sense that Tony was doing his best to preserve his patience. "You have a wonderful family now, indeed. And they will take you quite a ways. But then, know what?"

I shook my head, as best I could.

"You'll be alone," he said.

"Whatever. I could meet someo--"

"Maybe. So what? In this life, son, one thing is true: You wake up with yourself, and you fall asleep with yourself. Some will help you, some will harm you, most won't care one way or the other.

"So you kick butt in that manual chair. Good. And in the motor one. Good. But kid, you better learn that rules are rules, 'cause someday your parents'll tell you you have to go get a *job*, and I hope someday you even get a good one. But before you get good jobs, I guarantee you'll have to do some bad ones. And you'll have bosses who don't care about your condition. In fact, they'll be betting against you on account of it.

"And when they dish their rules, Tucker: You better be prepared to follow all of 'em."

With his grand speech concluded, Tony finally wheeled me back inside.

* * *

So much for living life one day at a time.

I still wasn't Tony's biggest fan, but at least now I was able to put all his behavior into context. As for his lesson, it made an impact, but it also left me with a burning question, one which I had no intention whatsoever of discussing with him:

Should one be a rule-follower or a rule-breaker?

I mean, look at me: I was now a total minority in life. I hadn't been born that way; I'd been born as a white male in a Christian upper middle class home. All stuff I had in common with many other people.

Being paralyzed was a whole other story.

Be that as it may, in light of my rare circumstances, maybe following rules really wasn't the best path to take. Maybe I should go the other way, not toward drugs and crime like Tony, but toward a little bit of rebellion. Going against the grain. Surprising those around me. Blowing people's minds.

Even dating Rebecca, or other girls like her...

Did that have to be so out of the question? According to the rule book, I now had to be an asexual guy in a chair who people looked away from in public.

But according to my new set of rules, I could do absolutely anything I wanted to.

In other words, there was the Tony route and there was the Alba route. Tony had his points, sure, but Alba had actually managed to set me free.

And she'd done so without giving speeches or getting into shouting matches.

Maybe it was 'cause I wasn't crazy about Tony, but our little trip to go see James didn't exactly have the effect he'd intended. I got the point, yeah, but I also learned a little about who I was. Sure, I was still just a kid, and I couldn't possibly have the entire picture, but I knew this much:

I didn't want to live my life doing what people expected of me.

* * *

I kept a close eye on my dad, meanwhile. His condition would have consumed all my thoughts, were it not for Rebecca's pending visit. In a way, I suppose his angels were looking out for him on that one.

Just as mine were looking out for me...

In any case, I think he toned down the drinking, or maybe stopped it altogether. I didn't detect any more sudden changes. He was generally his usual, uptight self. Not so tense as to be unpleasant, but not so loose as to seem inebriated.

Worked for me.

Meanwhile, getting back to my angels: Rebecca was showing up in twenty-four hours. I hadn't been this nervous – hadn't even felt this much emotion – since that moment on Friday the 13th when I'd woken up.

Every possible scenario raced through my mind:

Would it be a pity party, with her giving me sad, puppy dog eyes (the kind of eyes so many people around Colsen gave me, which made me crazy every single time)?

Would she be better able to navigate a conversation, or would I have to handle everything?

Would it last for two minutes or two hours?

Would I see her on Friday and Saturday or just on Friday? Was she even leaving on Saturday? Maybe Sunday?

Would my parents get the hint and leave her alone with me?

I had to still my mind somehow. Stop going in circles. I was sounding to myself like an unhinged maniac. She probably couldn't have guessed how much space her visit was taking up in my thoughts. From her point-of-view, I was probably so buried in my predicament that she was the last thing on my mind.

Should I play into that? How should I act?

I learned an invaluable life lesson while waiting for her to come: That human beings need other human beings as much as we need oxygen. Until then, I had taken the people I cared about for granted. And sure, my parents were the best, but it took the newness of Rebecca to drive this lesson home.

The newness, and – you know – the fact that she was *hot*.

Suddenly it was clear why Facebook and Twitter and all those other social media sites were popular. It's that human connection. That need to be heard, and to hear others. See others.

See Rebecca.

Twenty-four more hours.

* * *

I asked Reginald to comb my hair.

I would have asked my mother, but she was allegedly out pacing in the parking lot following a tiff with one of her instructors.

Great, I thought. They'll never let me out of here...

Maybe Rebecca would take me home. Maybe in some oddball twist of fate, she'd be the only one qualified to look after me, and everyone – our parents, the rehab people – would come to an agreement that I had to go and live with her.

Forever.

Now I was really thinking like a lunatic.

"Reggie," I asked, "can you comb my hair?"

Reggie was okay – at best. He was an orderly. He changed my sheets and my bedpan. Turned the TV on and off for me. Opened and closed the window shades.

And now I was asking him to comb my hair.

It wasn't ideal. I mean, the guy was a few notches below lukewarm, but I wasn't in a position to be picky here. I needed Rebecca to see not only the attractiveness I still retained, but some overall sense of stability and order.

She had to know I was strong.

Just like my parents.

Reggie looked at me. I couldn't read the look. It was somewhere between a scowl and a smirk. "You got a hot date?" he asked.

I breathed out some laughter. "Why does everybody say that?" I asked.

He laughed. It was kind of surprising, actually. And as he did so, he clapped his hands. Another good lesson learned in Colsen: Sometimes you just gotta break the ice to get people to stop acting cold.

"Who is she?" he wanted to know. "Girlfriend?"

"Friend."

"But a girl."

I looked at him. Nodded.

"Okay..." He started to look around the room. "Okay," he repeated, this time more to himself than me.

Then he disappeared for a while.

I found myself wondering whether he'd ever return. Man, I was starting to become some kind of a desperate psycho. His use of the word "okay" had been an agreement, right?

Right?

Moments turned to seconds. Seconds turned to minutes.

I found myself playing out Rebecca's visit inside my head. I tried not to – tried to push against it – but the more I resisted, the more it came.

Until Reggie came back again, and made me smile.

For dangling from the man's hand was a nice fat brush.

* * *

I felt crazy when I heard Rebecca was finally coming upstairs.

That's the only word to describe it. My mind wasn't working properly. I tried to form coherent thoughts, but none of them came out remotely comfortable.

Flat-out: I didn't even know who I was.

Forget about accidentally taking a bullet: This looming encounter was throwing me into a major tailspin. How would I act? How would I come off?

AUSTIN CHARTERS

Would she regret, in the end, having gone to all the trouble?

My mom was in the room with me. Dad's location was unknown for the moment, which was fine by me. Maybe he was out front, smoking a cigarette, waving the smoke away with his hand whenever a sick person got rolled by in a wheelchair.

He smoked, too, but that was only occasionally. At least, I think it was occasional. The way I understood it, he turned to cigarettes on those days when he was trying not to drink alcohol. Then again, who knew what he was really up to?

I forced my mind away from the old man. Time to focus on the young lady.

God. Did I just think that? "Young lady"?!

Like I said: *Crazy.*

I wanted to ask my mom to leave, but I figured she'd know to do so after Rebecca got settled. Or maybe she wouldn't. Maybe the tone in the room would be so awkward that my mom would suddenly take it upon herself to come to our rescue.

Now that would be really ugly. Excruciating, in fact.

Okay: It was really time for her to walk in now. The moments were easing by like syrup sliding down a plate.

"Mom?"

"Yeah?"

Her eyes had been aimed upward, toward the TV.

Some cheesy courtroom show. A lady with a loud purple sweatshirt was fighting with her landlord. I hadn't been paying too close attention, but I was kind of on the landlord's side.

Maybe it was just the woman's shirt.

"When Becky comes, can you--?"

But there she was.

In the doorway.

Like something straight out of my most amazing dream.

There before me. In the flesh. My girl. The one and only.

Rebecca.

* * *

Hopefully she hadn't heard me call her "Becky." I, for one, had no idea why I'd used that name with my mom. Maybe it had a way of making her sound more like a kid, and thus making the encounter sound more innocent, the better to assure my mom that there'd be no funny business when she took a hike.

Could you imagine? "Funny business"? Right there in Colsen?

It'd be the most joyful thing to take place there in forever, I can tell you that.

"Hi," I said to Rebecca.

She was frozen. Awkward.

Great. Here we go.

"Hi," she responded.

Her eyes were on me. She was taking me in. Yes, this is what a paralyzed person looks like. Here it is, real-as-real, right before your eyes.

A part of your own life.

She stepped into the room. My mom got up and extended a hand. "I'm Mrs. Frost," she said.

"Rebecca."

They shook hands.

I wondered why my mom had introduced herself as "Mrs. Frost." To all my guy friends, she was always "Paisley." What the hell was wrong with her?

Clearly, she'd made a key distinction between males and females.

Or maybe she was just being formal because we were in a hospital setting? Nah, I doubt that. Her gaze was screaming, *Female!*

My mom wouldn't be, like, competitive, would she? Hopefully not, 'cause she was about to take one long and serious walk.

"Mom, can you--?"

Phew. She got the message. Already, before I even formed the whole sentence, her hands were up and her feet were moving toward the door.

"You two have a good time catching up," she said.

And she was gone.

* * *

For a minute there, I found myself wondering whether I even really liked Rebecca.

Despite all the effort she'd put into coming up, her energy was as stiff as ever, if not more. An A for effort, sure, but in those first few minutes, she got a C for execution. She kept looking up at the TV. She asked some questions about what the hospital was like. I think she may have asked me how I was feeling.

No, scratch that. She didn't.

She asked how I was "doing." Slight difference there.

Or maybe I was being too hard on her. Maybe I'd built up the whole event so much that I was giving her a bad review just to protect myself from the blow of disappointment.

Perhaps I was better off just letting the whole thing take its course...

"That was really cool of you," I said. "To come."

"Oh, I... It's nothing."

"No. It really isn't."

Should I? Shouldn't I? What the hell...

"It means a lot to me."

She looked at me. I caught something in her look. Something deeper than she'd ever shown me. It's like when you go to a girl's house after school to study with her, 'cause the teacher paired you up or something, and you see her wearing sweatpants and no makeup for the first time.

In other words, you really *see* her.

And in that moment, after I said those words (which, by the way, had a pretty thorny and difficult journey from my vocal cords to my tongue), I felt I saw Rebecca for the very first time.

"Listen, um..."

Oh, no. I could feel it: She was about to say something...

Something important.

If I was wrong about this, then I had no intuition at all. And I seriously couldn't have no intuition, 'cause my head was now taking up more bandwidth than ever in my being.

"I feel bad," she said.

My eyebrows crunched together. "Bad about, like, what happened to me?"

"No. I mean, yes!"

We both laughed a little.

"But I feel bad – I was gonna say..."

A long and heavy moment creaked its way on by.

"...about how I acted before."

I thought back. Our times together. The cafeteria. So bright and crisp within the space of my mind's eye.

"I don't get it," I said.

But I did. I knew exactly what was about to come. And it gave me such a thrill I could have levitated.

She gave me full eye contact. Beautiful eyes. She went on, "I liked you. I mean: I *like* you. I still do. And I wanted to be with you. And I thought maybe you wanted to be with me. At lunch. I mean: more than at lunch. But when we ate together, I thought maybe that was going somewhere. But then it didn't.

"And that was all my fault."

I took a breath. Who was this person?

Whoever she was, I liked her, too.

"It wasn't your fault," I said, smiling. "It was both our faults. I was like stupid or something..."

"No!" She laughed. I think I spied a sparkle in her eye.

Was that a tear?

"You were doing everything," she said. "You were showing up. You know, I take Drama, and the teacher's, like, constantly talking about how we have to show up. Not only on stage, but in life. We have to be present.

"So that's why I came, Tucker.

"I wanted to show up for you.

"I wanted to show up and not, like, totally blow it this time."

* * *

That was it: She was crying.

And damn it, I'm not sure it was the right thing to do on my part, but I was crying, too. She reached out and touched my arm. I felt nothing. Then my hand.

She held my hand.

I felt it deep.

"That means a lot to me," I said.

Maybe I sounded corny; I don't know. But from what I understood about girls, their tolerance for corniness was well beyond what most guys could handle. So I was probably inside a reasonable safety zone.

So there I went, saying it again: "Means a lot."

She squeezed my hand. Then took a breath. The breath was loud there for a second, almost verging on a gasp, and I felt for certain that a weight had just slipped off her shoulders. She'd been rehearsing that. Building up just like I had, only I was just waiting around while she was planning and packing and driving and practicing her lines.

Or maybe the last part didn't go that far. But however much energy she'd put into her statement, she'd definitely nailed it.

And it was now pinned permanently against my heart.

* * *

We shelved the drama for the rest of the visit.

I kept thinking things would go deep again, like she had some other tearful confession stored away somewhere, but it was probably for the better that things stayed light. We watched TV. She helped me with lunch. I introduced her to my dad; he did okay. Was a little distant, but amply warm. Then Reggie came in to check on me, and made fun of me about how I'd asked him to comb my hair. Under other circumstances – like if the tone in the room had stayed tight and awkward – him being open about that might have annoyed me, but right then, in light of Rebecca's confession, it all worked just fine. I was happy to have her know I'd been looking forward to her visit enough to throw some extra effort at my hair. And she laughed freely at Reggie's remarks, and I sat there all proud of myself for how I'd managed to finally break the ice with that guy.

By the time she left, I could see the sky getting purplish through the window. I lied there praying that she'd kiss me...and she did, only on the cheek, which was plenty for that particular visit. When she left, I found myself watching her body, my eyes taking in her features, and wondering if I could someday, somehow, know that body. Like – did she like me *that* much? How far would it go?

Or would I remain her friend? The shot she'd missed?

Her living, breathing regret?

* * *

As the sky got dark, so did my mood.

I found myself wandering around a shadowy maze within my mind. I even tried to doze off to escape the murk, but sleep wasn't coming – I'd been too excited about seeing her. Too much adrenaline had made its way through my bloodstream.

So I lied in bed thinking about my future. That was a deathly avenue for my mind to take. Since the day I'd woken up, the staff members at both places kept reminding me that I was now in "one day at a time" mode. Just let each day take care of itself. Take each one as it comes, and don't try to live all your tomorrows at the same time.

But right now, that was becoming impossible.

I loved Rebecca. I didn't care how crazy the thought was. Sure, I barely knew her, but we'd already bonded on so many levels. Just the fact that she'd come...she'd given us an experience. We'd been through something together.

Cried together.

Her hand on my hand.

Her lips on my cheek.

But could I know her all the way? What could I offer in that regard? I mean, she was hot – almost all the guys at school had an eye on her. How could I of all people compete against them?

The things they could do with her, that I couldn't.

My world got heavy. The future – the one they'd warned me never to look right in the eye – was filled with shrieking terror. I tried to comfort myself with the thought that maybe I had some advantage *because* of my predicament. Maybe my vulnerability made me attractive.

Hell, maybe Rebecca was a dominant type, and I could be her submissive partner.

That made me smile a little, but the smile didn't go in all the way. The truth was, the damn accident had effectively lopped off a giant piece of my life. Something most everybody else got to enjoy had been ripped away from me inside a single moment.

It wasn't fair.

Yeah, yeah – life wasn't fair. I'd always known that. My father had only been sure to remind me, like, 10,000 times.

But I'd been flung into a deep swamp of unfairness.

And I stayed up 'til about 3AM that night, wondering if I'd ever manage to crawl my way out.

* * *

She came back for breakfast.

We went to the cafeteria together. No irony there, ha-ha. Just like the old days. As of yet, I hadn't really ventured beyond my room too much. But her presence made me feel more mobile, kind of like a tour guide. Like when guests come to visit your hometown, and you end up going to half a dozen places you never saw before, just to make them happy.

Of course, my "hometown", for now, was Colsen, and it wasn't the most luxurious place on Earth, but I doubted that Rebecca was going to hold that against me.

As we ate, I wanted to talk about the future. My

parents were making headway in their coursework, so my day of (relative) freedom wasn't far away. Could even be less than a couple of weeks.

So everything in me wanted to discuss when I'd see Rebecca again.

But I didn't do it. I stuck with – not exactly small talk, but nothing too intense or major. I kept telling myself that she'd made the trip, and that, along with the prior day's chat, were enough for the time being.

After all, the last thing I wanted to do was force the discussion in the wrong direction and end up parting with her on unhappy terms. I mean, the day before had been perfectly happy, and I'd still managed to kick myself to sleep in a state of despair.

So I really had no choice but to take it slow.

Which was kind of fitting, I thought with an inward smirk, for a guy in my position.

Over breakfast, I pointed out some other patients, whispered to her about their stories. There was Clyde, an old-timer who'd also had a gun accident, only in his case he'd been the one to pull the trigger, and as a result he'd lost an entire leg. Worse off was Sheila, some 20 years our senior, who'd been on a bus where the driver fell asleep. He went barreling down a damn hillside. Three people were killed. Most of the living walked away with cuts and scrapes. But Sheila occupied a middle position, and was now fully paralyzed from the neck down.

"I'm luckier than her," I whispered to Rebecca.

ROLLING HOME

Rebecca gave me another one of those looks: the-girl-in-her-house-without-makeup look. "You are?" she asked. "I mean..."

Right away, I could tell she regretted her wording. But I didn't hold it against her. It was entirely clear to me by now that people who weren't in my position tended to trip all over themselves when trying to communicate with people who were.

"Totally," I said, my tone firm and clear. "I've got my arms. I've got my youth."

I meant it, too, even though I sensed some skepticism in Rebecca's gaze. One thing Colsen gave to me, amidst all its grimness, was perspective on the fact that no matter how far I fell, somebody would always be lower. I guess technically that meant that somewhere on this planet there had to be *some* person who was the absolute lowest, but I was thankful for the fact that that guy wasn't me.

"Did you ever hear that story?" I asked Rebecca. "About the people holding their problems in bags?"

She thought about it. "No." She shook her head.

"Well, it's not really like a story-story," I said. "It's more like a metaphor. See, there's a room full of people, and they're all told to put all of their problems into bags. Then they're all directed to put their bags in the middle of the room, and each person is encouraged to pick up somebody else's bag. They then have a choice: either they can go home with their own bag or somebody else's.

"In the end, everybody goes back to their own bag."

Yet again, unexpectedly, I saw a flash of tears in Rebecca's eyes.

"That's so beautiful," she said.

"Yeah."

"Do you think it's true-to-life? That we'd all prefer our own shit over someone else's?"

I took a moment to think about it. My dad had told me the metaphor back in the hospital. From the second I'd heard it, I just accepted it as a basic human truth. But now Rebecca was making me take another look.

Still, I landed in the same spot:

"Definitely," I said.

"No matter what?"

"No matter what." I took a pause. "See, not every problem is really just a problem. Life's not that simple. Everything in life has positive and negative aspects to it. So when you have a problem, you get stuff out of it. You learn about life. You learn who you are."

After a nod, Rebecca asked me, "What's something positive you've gotten out of your problem?"

I looked in her eyes. Gave her a smile. I couldn't help myself, venturing full-on into corny territory again:

"I'm looking at it," I said.

* * *

ROLLING HOME

My dad wheeled me out to the curb to say goodbye to Rebecca. I kind of wished somebody else – preferably a staff member – had been around to do so, because even though I knew my dad was trying to give us our space, I sensed him judging every aspect of our inter-action.

And Rebecca must have sensed it, too, 'cause she didn't even kiss me goodbye again. The only kiss I would get from her during that weekend was the one from Friday afternoon. I kept replaying it in my mind, and then started wondering if anything like it would ever happen again.

Much less anything *beyond* it.

My dad had a perfect way of making things worse. For starters, once her cab back to her hotel pulled away, he didn't even stand there so I could watch it go. I mean: Isn't that part of the process? You watch the car pull away, then even share a wave with the person who's leaving?

Apparently Dad never got the memo on that one, 'cause he just turned me right around to leave. And I didn't have the energy or comfort required to ask him to stay for just an extra moment.

But he made things even worse than that as he wheeled me back up toward my room. For that's when he said to me, "Nice of your friend to come and visit."

I swore I could hear him putting extra emphasis on "friend."

'Cause I knew the type of guy he was. He was a

logical type, and worse than that, he was a logical type whom life had beaten down. So he tended to steer clear of dreaming and romanticizing.

A lot of the time, I prayed that I never turned out like that.

And jeez, now look at me: Life had certainly dished me a nice, hard beating.

As for my dad, I think by putting some extra seasoning on the word "friend", he was trying to be a good and dutiful father...and effectively trying to keep my hopes good and low. But what he didn't understand was that hope was all I had right then. And I'm not talking about vague, fantasy-type hope. I'm talking about an actual anticipation of a good outcome.

I needed to be with Rebecca.

I needed that weekend at Colsen to not be the last time I ever saw her.

CHAPTER 4

Waiting

O kay. Easy does it.
This is simple.
It's...just...a...can...of...soda...

I'd already managed to pick up soda cans in between both hands, but on this day I was intent upon doing it with one hand. It was a reasonably good item for testing out my single-handed ability. Not too large and bulky, but still with a smooth, borderline slick surface...

The kind that makes it easy to drop.

It had been two weeks since I'd been discharged from Colsen. Since returning home, my life had become a very functional state of affairs. Learning how to do this and that. Learning how to be a person again.

Learning how...to pick up soda cans...

I took my time. Breathed in and out.

Back at Colsen, there'd been this old lady whose name I couldn't remember, who talked my mother's ear off about meditation. She was way into it, apparently. How she ever managed to meditate – or achieve any calmness whatsoever – in that place was a mystery, but just the same, that's what she did.

And right now, whoever she was, she was my inspiration.

I had no choice but to be calm and patient. Urgency and irritability would not only break me, but they'd destroy my whole family. We didn't all need a storm at our center. I didn't feel this way 'cause I was a saint, but because I really needed my life to function well on some level.

It seemed obvious that being a basket case was not the best path to functionality.

Okay...Breathe in, breathe out...Easy does it...

I reached out. My hands made kind of natural hooks. The thumbs and index fingers were positioned in just such a way where between the two of them, they could produce some primitive version of a grip.

I set the can within that grip. Tried to pick it up.

Nope. Too sloppy. The can tipped over and rolled across the kitchen table. Fortunately, I trapped it under my wrist before it hit the ground. My mom was in the living room, and I would have felt bad asking her to come and pick it up.

Using both hands, I straightened it back up on the tabletop.

I shut my eyes. In my own personal darkness, I asked God to let me pick up the soda can with one hand. All around the world, billions of people prayed for love, health, peace, joy, and money, and here I was just asking to be able to lift a can.

Shouldn't have been too much to ask, I figured.

I'd been raised religious, but just the same, I didn't always address God one-on-one. I wasn't like some members of our church who claimed to be in regular dialogue with the man upstairs. I still prayed, however. And I bought the idea that God had a plan. And that my current circumstances, however difficult, were just a challenging aspect of that plan.

As I sat with my eyes closed, I picked up on a little peace of wisdom. I can't say for certain that it was God talking to me; maybe it was just my memories of overhearing that old lady go on about meditation.

In any case, the wisdom was to not put any thought into the motion. Just let my body, whatever its limitations, do what it needed to.

That was the key.

Stay pure, stay clean.

I opened my eyes. The kitchen light seemed loud. Like my inner world was being invaded.

Still, I kept my nerves nice and cool. No thoughts; I combed them all away. This moment was devoted entirely to action.

I blinked once. Eyed the can. So daunting for me; so simple for others.

Then I reached out and picked it up.

* * *

It was perfect!

I called my mom. She could tell from the excitement in my voice that this was important. "Wow, Tucker!" she said, entering the room. "Way to go!"

"I know! I couldn't even do it just yesterday."

"One day at a time, right?"

With my eyes, I gave her something resembling a nod.

There was only one problem, though. "Mom?" I said.

"Yeah?" She'd already angled her body toward the fridge to grab something while she was there. Now she was turning back my way, eyebrows raised, hands on her hips.

"I, um..."

I blushed. I held up the can.

She sighed. I could feel how much love she had for me.

"Oh, Tucker," she said. "We should've opened it first!"

The two of us laughed. She walked on over. Making sure to keep the soda can secure in my grip, she reached around to its top and snapped it open. A little bit spilled out, ran down my hand.

Didn't matter. I slurped off the fizz, then gulped down a couple of swallows.

Hissing out a breath, I said, "Thanks."

As she walked back toward the fridge, she said, "Don't mention it."

I looked at her from behind. Silently, my eyes tearing up, I thanked God for giving me this woman to be my mother.

* * *

"I want to work out my arms," I said.

It seemed that every time I spoke with a doctor, my arms became the central topic of conversation. To me, this made sense, since I still had them available to me. Be that as it may, it was kind of depressing that I always had to be the first one to bring it up.

The local physician's name was Dr. Briggs. From the moment he walked into the examination room, I got a bad vibe. Almost like he was too stiff.

Like he'd been *preparing* for this encounter.

Not a good sign.

See, with spinal cord injuries, the social aspect of the patient's encounters with his or her doctors colors every other aspect. If the doctor's even the slightest bit tense or not accustomed to people in wheelchairs, the resulting communication issues become so distracting that it's hard to really talk about important things.

Such as, on that particular day – my 7th day out of Colsen – the issue of my arms...

"I'm not so sure about that," said Dr. Briggs.

I looked at my dad. Since it was a Saturday, he'd volunteered to take me. My mom was always a better bet, but I had to hand it to him for at least being interested. Right now, however, his presence was proving to be the very disappointment I'd expected it to be. Which is to say that he seemed to be in agreement with the doctor's words. Either that or he was nodding his head for no reason whatsoever.

"How come?" I asked Dr. Briggs, looking back at him.

"Tucker," said my dad, "be patient."

I didn't feel impatient. I thought I sounded fine. Why was my dad seeking drama when there was none?

Doing his best to ignore my dad, Dr. Briggs said, "Since your arms are in good shape, we should treat them gently."

"I'm young," I said. "There are wheelchair sports. I've seen people on the Internet with arms as big as wrestlers'."

"Let's take our time," said the doctor. He then turned to my dad. "Go easy on the arms," he advised. "And I'll see you in two more weeks. So long."

Briggs rushed his way out the door. My father said goodbye, with a little wave.

I chose not to.

ROLLING HOME

* * *

"There's no reason for it!"

We were in the car, headed to a hamburger place, hence my willingness to yell and scream as loud as I wanted.

"Tucker..."

"No! Don't 'Tucker' me. I know my body. I'm in my body. I'm still here. Still alive. Do you guys, like, want no part of me to function a hundred percent?"

"Don't be ridiculous." I felt my father's tension. He was clearly trying to calculate just how dramatic this particular discussion would become...

"I'm *not* being ridiculous. These doctors are horrible. Like 3 percent of them understand what I'm actually going through."

"Then we'll get a second opinion, Tucker!"

"Good! And a third opinion, and a fourth opinion, until I'm doing 100 push-ups a day..."

Now I was *certainly* being ridiculous, but I had to exaggerate to get my point across.

* * *

The poor waitress at the hamburger joint caught me on the wrong day...

Our family had always gone there. Now with my injury, though, the staff always greeted us like newcomers. No inquiries. No expressions of concern. Just the thin, absurd put-on that they had no idea who we were.

My dad seemed fine with this; he didn't want to get into it.

Me? Not so fine; not so much.

"Hi," said the waitress, chirping like a bird, "how may I help you today?"

Not only was she chirping, she was looking 1,000 percent at my dad, as though he were the only person at our table.

As though, by extension, he was the only one capable of ordering.

"My son will have the--"

"No, I'll order," I said.

I flicked my eyes up at her. Come on, look, I said inside my head. Take a look. This is real. This is the planet you live on.

She had no choice. She turned and eyed me.

And suddenly all her chirpy-birdy nonsense had evaporated. She was as cold as James's nights in the alleyway. "What will you have?" she asked, as though she and I were old, sworn enemies.

"Burger. Cheese. Bacon. Fries. Large coke."

She scribbled it all down.

"And maybe a little respect?" I added.

"Tucker!" My dad's face was every known shade of red.

"Excuse me?" asked the waitress.

"You'll have to forgive my son, he's..."

"I'm what?"

"You're fine," she said, scooping up our menus. "You're both fine."

When she was gone, my dad aimed a finger at me: "You will apologize to her. You will apologize, and you will be sincere."

"Why?" I asked him. "So everything can be cool on the surface but crappy underneath? The way you like it?"

He backed up a little in his seat. I'd clearly wounded him. That only pleased me for half a second, after which I just sat there feeling like the biggest jerk on the planet.

We sat there in silence 'til she returned with our food. I had to give her credit for actually doing so, and not handing off the chore to another server. Prior to her appearance, while seething, I repeated to myself over and over that I absolutely would not apologize. After all, *she* had been the one who'd been rude...

But when she arrived, my heart sang a different tune. Instinctively, I let the words roll out: "Hey look, I'm sorry. I'm just...going through a lot..."

She smiled at me. But her eyes were sad. Blinking, and therefore producing a tear or two, she said, "You don't have to be sorry. You two enjoy your meal."

My dad looked at me after she went. He smiled.

I gathered up my breath and smiled back.

AUSTIN CHARTERS

* * *

Two whole weeks had gone by since I'd come home.

Me? I became something of a student. A student of existence, and not in the philosophical sense. No, I was just a guy learning how to be in the world. How to get my teeth brushed. Make my way through a shower. Go to the bathroom in an efficient manner.

Interacting with people was a whole other thing. I found out pretty quick, once we were settled back at home, that two kinds of reactions tended to dominate people's responses to me...

The first one was, they'd start communicating with me as though my *brain* had been the part of me that got cracked. Ironic, since my brain, aside from some frustration and anxiety, was operating absolutely fine. Just the same, it wasn't abnormal to find myself being addressed in a sing-song type of voice:

"How-are-you?"

These sing-songers (or song-singers? I really don't know what to call those fools) always worked real hard to sound an audible note of compassion in their voices. Like, *"Oh, you poor thing."*

And maybe they even meant well – I'm sure most of them did. But unless somebody's still a toddler, that note of communication won't go down very well, no matter who's on the receiving end.

Pretty quickly, I got in the habit of cracking as confident and charismatic a smile as possible to these people and just saying, "I'm fine. You can talk to me normal."

My mom often laughed when I replied that way.

My dad, well – not so much. More for him was letting out windy sighs.

As for the second group, they somehow managed to be even worse. These were the people who got all inward around me. Maybe they didn't think I noticed, but I tended to notice most every time. Their faces would tighten. Their eyes would get far away. The net impression they gave out was one of anger, but I certainly hope my presence didn't make them angry! I think that reaction, like the sing-song one, was just driven by basic awkwardness.

Then again, who knows? Maybe the sight of a paralyzed person *does* drum up anger. After all, it puts people in touch with their own vulnerability. It's a little message from the universe, reminding people that they're not made of steel.

In general, I've learned that people can't stand the reminder.

Overall, it was very rare to encounter somebody who didn't miss a beat in my presence. Someone who just rolled with it, absorbed the reality of my humanity, and managed to act as though the sky wasn't falling in my presence.

One such person, naturally, was Rebecca...

* * *

But two weeks had gone by, and she hadn't called.

I thought of calling her, but was honestly afraid of putting that card into play. It was like having an ace in my hand; if I let it go, I might never see it again.

And then what?

What would I have to looking forward to then?

My other friends had taken a hard position: For the most part, they weren't coming around. Double Mike was now a thing of the past. Some friends of the family did stop by, and even some friends of my brother, but nobody I really hung with before the accident.

I was starting to feel kind of alone.

Rebecca.

I needed her. If I called and things didn't go anywhere, I would certainly roll over into a pretty deep abyss. Then again, maybe she was waiting for my call. Maybe giving me my space, in light of the natural adjustment I was undergoing.

But to hell with that. My life had to be about something more than making sure my teeth were brushed and my toilet was flushed. I was still human – and in many ways more so than ever before.

My emotions, in other words, were at the wheel.

My heart, though I couldn't feel it physically, was pretty much running the show at that point. And it was gunning for companionship, and ideally love, at every turn.

* * *

I decided to bring it up with Jordan. If I couldn't talk *to* Rebecca, then the best I could do was talk *about* her. So one night, after our parents were asleep, when I heard him walking by in the hall, I called him over:

"Jordan?"

"Yeah?"

"I need to talk to you."

His body stiffened. He and I hadn't had anything resembling a full-blown conversation since that day out on the mountain. He hesitated for a moment, then walked into my room with the ease of an employee being monitored by his supervisor...

"What's up?"

"Can you shut the door?"

So he turned around and did so. Then he locked it. Then he unlocked it.

Great, he was every bit as awkward as the next guy. I actually laughed a little, but he didn't catch it. He sat down beside me on my bed and repeated his previous question: "What's up?"

"I need your advice."

He squinted at me. I read his look to be asking, How could I possibly give YOU advice? But the truth was, he could. He was good with girls. Always dating someone. It seemed to come pretty naturally to him, as though he were fulfilling some basic need. He didn't get caught up in all the chatter and strategy crap that so many guys wandered into.

Like myself, for example, inside my own head.

"There's that girl..."

"Rebecca?" he asked.

Right then, I knew that he'd discussed her with my parents. God only knew how far that discussion went. Did the three of them gather around shaking their heads, hoping against hope that that pretty girl didn't break their poor boy's heart?

"Yeah. See, she came to see me up there. She cried and shit. Said she liked me."

"She said that?"

He wasn't sounding a note of condescension. On the contrary, he seemed delighted – and more relaxed than he had since I'd spotted him in the hallway. Maybe it was a revelation to him, that a girl could actually like me.

After all, it had been to me.

"Yeah. But the question is: How much?"

He nodded. Seemed to be devoting some serious thought to the matter. He gave his lower lip a brief chew with his upper teeth, then released it and asked, "Were you together before?"

"No."

"But you were friends."

"Yeah. And it was like we were almost about to be together. But then I blew it. It sort of stalled."

"Whose idea was it for her to come see you?"

I had a feeling he already knew it was her, but in any case, I just said, "Hers."

"Then she comes up there crying and says she likes

you?"

By way of my eyelids and facial muscles, I gave him a nod.

He touched my leg. "Pretty far drive. I'd say she could have serious intentions."

I felt my spirit accelerate. My breath was quickening. "Okay," I said, "but she hasn't called. And I'm afraid if I call her, I'll blow it, and then I'm, like, out of prospects."

"Plenty of fish in the sea, bro."

He winked at me. But he didn't mean that. We both knew I had to take this prospect seriously. Plenty of fish, sure – but we seemed to have a rare and exotic one on our hook. Or my hook, anyway.

"So do I call her?"

"Of course."

"Why 'of course'? It's been two weeks; she never called me."

"Tucker..."

We made lengthy eye contact. I couldn't remember the last time I'd had such a good look at my bro's face.

"...there's something you have to understand..."

"Okay," I said.

I expected him to launch into some sort of lecture about how the female mind operates – some sort of a complex playboy philosophy about the chase, complete with cat and dog metaphors – but instead he said something truly surprising:

"You're intimidating, man."

I had to take a moment there. "You mean, like, how? As a person?"

"No. Well, yeah. That, too. You're a good-looking guy. Takes one to know one, of course."

I laughed.

"So that made you kind of intimidating before. Good looks'll do that. But I'm talking about your situation. It scares people."

"So then I *shouldn't* call her?"

"No! Stupid. That's exactly why you SHOULD call her. What do you have rocks in your head?"

I thought it over. His meaning sunk in. Regardless, he went ahead and verbalized it:

"She's keeping her distance because she doesn't know what reality is like for you. For all she knows, you're wide awake screaming every night."

The two of us laughed at this.

"So you have to take the initiative, bro. You have to show her that you're a safe place. In fact, she's probably just leaving you alone right now."

"Yeah, that crossed my mind."

He slapped my shin and stood up. "Let me know how it goes," he said, then started walking toward the door.

As he shut it behind him, I felt my nerves start chewing each other to pieces. Did he really expect me to call her right then? No, he couldn't expect that. I mean, in light of my arm motion, I did have some ability to dial a phone number. Even though my fingers were stiff, I could angle them to press the buttons, then keep the phone inside my hand and...

No.

That was enough work for today.

The call would have to wait 'til tomorrow.

* * *

It was a school day, so I let the hours slip by, not wanting to call her before she was home. My tutor came by for a three-hour stretch in the morning. It was pretty amazing how fast time flew when I was the only student, with one-on-one instruction. The tutor's name was Mrs. Brass, and she was a jolly old lady with super-wide hips. She was one of the few who didn't seem to think my condition was anything worth reacting to, and I loved her for it, but then again that was all part of her job. She'd been trained for it. So major points went to her, definitely, but she couldn't touch my dear, sweet, awesome Rebecca in the purity department.

Mrs. Brass left right as my mom came home from shopping. Even though my dad didn't want her spoiling me, she always brought me little gifts – movies and music and chocolate snacks. Physical items were a cumbersome thing, and I was far better off consuming digital content (even digital food would have come as a relief), but her intention made each gift an occasion for a smile.

She had me smiling almost daily.

Before 3PM, my selected time for calling Rebecca, Mom fed me a dozen teaspoons of chocolate pudding, so by the time the Moment of Truth arrived, I was feeling a little hyper, even manic.

I wasn't quite sure if this was good or bad.

Before I dialed, I'd lied in bed for over 20 minutes. I held a silent conversation with myself about courage. The thing about courage is, I told myself, it doesn't come cheap. You have to *earn* it. And that means doing the stuff you dread. For once you do it, you graduate, and get a Medal of Courage pinned to your chest.

But if you do nothing, you get nothing.

Just more fear.

And I didn't want to grow into a fear-oriented person. Truthfully, I couldn't afford to, not in my position. Fear was death. I for one still had plenty of life inside me.

So with that thought in mind, I dialed Rebecca.

She answered during the second ring. From the minute go, her tone alerted me to the fact that she was thrilled.

Better than thrilled.

Relieved, she was.

I have no recollection of what we said. I just remember the excitement underneath her words. And before I knew it, we'd made plans to get together that coming Saturday.

* * *

ROLLING HOME

Getting in and out of the car was a chore.

How it worked was, someone would wheel me to the vehicle. Then that person would create a bridge between me and the car using what's called a sliding board. It looked a little like a surfboard; this slick sheet of plastic which, once my butt was on it, ushered me down into the car. It was like going on a slide, but for only one second. In the beginning, the process of getting me into or out of a vehicle could easily eat up 20 minutes – maybe more. But the more we did it, the faster it moved.

Which was good by me, as I intended to go see Rebecca as much as possible.

The car ride over lasted about a thousand years. My dad did the driving, and his energy was so thick I could practically *see* it. Was he uptight about me seeing Rebecca? Wasn't that *her* parents' job? The parents of the boy have nothing to fear.

Only this guy obviously was afraid of me being let down.

"How much time do you need?" he asked me as we pulled up her driveway.

"I don't know. Three hours? I'll call you."

"Okay." He threw the car into park. I prayed with all my might that he'd just get out and then help me do the same, but I sensed correctly that he wanted to engage me in a talk. "And Tucker..." he said.

Here it comes...

"Don't let her play games, y'know?"

I skipped right past amusement, right past awkwardness, right past aggravation, and right into full-fledged anger:

"What is that supposed to mean?"

"Nothing. Rebecca's great. Just...girls be can tricky."

"Tricky is well within the realm of what I can handle, Dad."

"I know. You're a strong guy." Somehow the compliment didn't touch me. "But this is..."

He didn't want to say what he wanted to say. Fine by me, 'cause I didn't want to hear it. It was no doubt some sort of warning in regard to how strange this girl must have been to have wanted to be around a guy like me.

And that was the last thing I needed to hear.

"...it's new territory. Know what I mean?"

"I'll be fine, Dad."

If able to, I would have kicked the floor beneath me.

My anger stayed lit up for a good few minutes. The whole sliding board process didn't make it better. Add to that the annoyance of being wheeled to her door, and I showed up feeling pretty pissed off at the world.

Fortunately, my future bore brighter notes.

For within the next hour, Rebecca would make me feel a whole lot better...

CHAPTER 5

Rising

O f all the things that could have happened when I went into Rebecca's house, the last thing I would have expected was to think about Tony...

He hadn't really been on my mind since Colsen. In fact, Tony was the sort of guy you kind of try to forget about when he's not right in front of you. However, after I said hello to Rebecca's mom, Trish (nice lady, no awkwardness, said she'd "heard a lot of good things" about me, which was nice), Rebecca rapidly put me in mind of my old rehab "coach."

"I have questions for you," she said to me.

We were in her living room. It wasn't as private as I'd hoped for, but at least her TV – which was pretty huge, with an 80-inch screen – was on. That provided a buffer between us and Trish, who was mostly in the kitchen and at times walking up and down the nearest hallway. I was in my chair, facing the TV. Rebecca was seated on the couch, with her legs tucked underneath her body. I liked seeing her that way; she looked informal.

I liked everything about her, in fact.

"Okay," I answered. "Ask me anything."

See, what Tony had taught me – and it was actually, in retrospect, a pretty good lesson – was that when you go on a job interview, the smart thing to do is to ask at least as many questions as you answer. He had brought this up one day as we made our rounds, in the midst of one of his speeches about having the right attitude or something. The point was that asking questions gave you control over the conversation. It doesn't seem that way on the surface, but once you try it out, it becomes undeniable.

For questions open doors. Questions expand horizons. "Curious people ask questions," said Tony. People who are closed off and shut down don't.

It came as a relief to me that Rebecca had questions. Otherwise, we risked slipping into the same awkwardness that had haunted us too many times before.

And I was game. When I said, "Ask me anything", I meant it.

"Seriously," I went on. "I don't care. I'm okay talking about it."

"How do you shower?" she asked.

"Sponge baths, lots of the time. And my parents installed a seat in my shower."

"What about the bathroom?"

"I have this bag..." I pointed it out to her. "And a bedpan. Sometimes it's on the toilet like a regular person."

We both laughed.

"What about...?"

Uh oh. She was angling her head to peek out into the hallway. Was this actually headed where I thought it was?

I hoped so.

She aimed a finger down at her own crotch. Just seeing her do that spun my world around. "Do you work down there?"

"I do," I said.

The words came out lightning fast. The truth was, though, that I was bluffing. I had no idea whether or not I still worked down there. Sometimes in the morning, I'd wake up with an erection, but to my knowledge that wasn't the same as being able to function with a girl. Meanwhile, since my hands weren't able to grip things easily, I was limited in terms of experimenting on my own.

So I didn't know. But for now, for me, it was worth believing that my answer was correct.

Moreover, I caught her eyes when I answered. She

liked that answer, no doubt about it. I mean: Who asks that question if they're only curious?

No: We weren't in Tony-job-interview territory anymore.

This was a good notch or two (or three) beyond curiosity.

Rebecca had deeper things in mind.

* * *

At the risk of sounding corny, I have to say that she saved my life.

Just her interest in me alone kept me out of the abyss. I can't imagine what would have filled the void had she not been there around that time in my life. Truth be told, I can only thank God for sending her to comfort me. Whether she knew it or believed it or not, Rebecca was on an angel's mission.

She was keeping this-here boy from being overtaken by too much darkness.

She didn't revisit the sexual question right away. She did, however, start talking about having kids. The topic seemed to be on her mind a little beyond what one might expect from a girl in high school. This conveyed to me that her talking about kids was really a way of talking about sex.

'Cause she asked me more than once if I wanted to have any.

Instinctively, I had to say no. Much as I loved my

parents, and as much as they had given me, I couldn't picture myself raising a kid. How would that work out, logistically?

The good news was, Rebecca said she didn't want any, either.

That first day with her shined bright in my memory. It was just us in the living room for three or four hours, but on account of her questions, the conversation flowed fine – and when it didn't there was always something on the TV to remark on or make fun of.

By the time my dad came, the sun was down. He took mercy on me: He didn't ask me a single question about how it had gone. In a way, this kind of hurt me; I wished there was more ease between us. On the other hand, our last attempt at visiting the topic of Rebecca hadn't yielded much fruit.

So on the ride home, he talked about The Beatles instead. The radio station he had on was playing a marathon of some kind: one Beatles song after another. His commentary sounded like pure chatter at first – just an old guy reminiscing about his generation's most popular music – but he did say something that sunk in deep with me:

"They evolved after a while," he told me.

"How's that?"

"If you notice, their early tunes were very cheery and innocent. Still great, but not as deep. Then later, they got heavier. Darker. It had more soul."

I thought about it. He was right. "Wasn't that 'cause they, like, got into drugs? Isn't Lucy in the Sky with Diamonds all about LSD?"

The two of us had to laugh.

"Maybe," he said, clearly punting. "But however they got there, they got there."

He threw the switch, turned the volume up. No *way* he was about to pursue that discussion with me, nor I with him.

Drugs didn't matter. That wasn't anything I wanted to go near. What mattered was his overriding point, which was that they'd started at A and gone to Z.

And if I wanted this life of mine to work out, then I had to dig in and be willing to do the same thing.

* * *

Two weeks later, after a pretty solid string of visits to Rebecca's (at least twice each week, with a third visit thrown in at the mall, and one visit turning into two after she drove me home one night and stuck around my house for a couple hours), she dove right back into her favorite topic:

"I lied," she said.

We were in her bedroom. That destination got established around the third visit. Her parents didn't seem to care at all. After all, what was this kid in a wheelchair capable of doing?

Little did they know...

"What did you lie about?" I asked her.

We were on the floor, bodies balancing atop and in between a whole bunch of colorful pillows. She'd gotten pretty good at helping me in and out of my chair. We had our sloppy moments, like one when she stepped on my toe and we spent 20 minutes trying to figure out if she'd broken it (she hadn't), but in general, she got the job done.

"Having kids..." she said.

I sucked in some breath. Where was *this* talk going? She wasn't about to tell me that she had a kid somewhere, was she? Great. The last thing I needed was for her to say, "Meet, Jimmy!", then introduce me to some three-year-old boy who'd been waiting in the next room...

Fortunately, nothing like that happened.

"What do you mean?" I asked.

"I do want to have them."

"Okay," I said. "That's fine with me."

What in the world was this girl talking about? I just couldn't wrap my mind around her strategy. She definitely wasn't suggesting that we were capable of getting married; that was beyond premature, to say the least. So even though I'm a guy and I'm regularly guilty of having erotic things in my brain, I had to conclude that her constant visiting of this topic had to do with sex.

'Cause what else could be underneath it?

I supposed, in that moment, that there was really only one way to find out:

"Why do you keep, like, bringing this up?"

She giggled. Looked away. Put her palm against her mouth.

"Are you asking me to be the father of your child?"

This question made her crack up laughing. It wasn't all out of humor, though, 'cause when her smile made way for a regular expression, I could see that her face had been overtaken by a blush.

"It's on my mind a lot lately," she said, as if that explained anything.

"But why? And why would I care if you lied? It's okay with me either way, like..."

I let my point hang in the air. Just throwing out my fishing line, waiting for a bite.

She sat up and pushed her hair back from her shoulders. Looking down at me, she said, "I don't have anybody else to talk about it with."

"You're not really doing a good job of explaining..."

"I just..." She threw her hands up, briefly. "...like talking to you about things I can't talk about with anyone else."

Then just-like-that, she swooped down and kissed me.

Her lips were so soft, I couldn't believe it. The texture didn't seem entirely human. It lasted for several moments – long ones. She didn't give me her tongue, but it was right there, not too far behind her lips, poking out just slightly and sweetening the contact.

When she backed up, she smiled.

My jaw hung for half a second, then I recovered. I couldn't believe it.

I was happy she'd been the one to do it, 'cause I was certainly at a disadvantage when it came to leaning in. Logistically speaking, the duty fell entirely on her.

And she'd followed through.

I smiled back.

This was happening, now.

It was real.

* * *

"Got a girlfriend, huh?"

This was Grandpa Angus talking.

God works in mysterious and yet, somehow, very coherent ways. I hadn't seen much of Angus since the accident. It wasn't that we were keeping our distance – at least not on the surface. It was more a matter of me being so tied up in matters of rehabilitation, and matters of Rebecca, that there just wasn't much available time.

Plus – yeah – we both understood that facing each other would not be easy.

Ironically, though, I had an easier time around him, the man who pulled the trigger, than I did around my dad. As for the God part of the equation, it worked out that I started seeing more of Grandpa Angus at just around the same time as things started picking up with Rebecca.

Almost as though God knew not to put us back together until something positive was happening with me.

Now it most certainly was. Not only that, but it gave me and Grandpa something solid to talk about. He wasn't like my dad in this regard. He liked the topic of Rebecca. He loved that she made me happy, and that in turn made him happy.

More than ever, in a way, I loved my grandpa. Somehow the tragedy that now hung between us had brought us closer.

By the grace of God, I guess...

"Who told you that?" I asked, playing the role of the shy kid. Truth was, I was more than happy to get into this topic. My brother was already sick of hearing about it, and there was no way I'd go near it with my parents.

Still, I couldn't just jump right in...

We were in Grandpa's garage; he was fixing his truck. He'd invited me to come over and "help out", whatever that meant. I certainly couldn't hand him a wrench. What I could do, however, was not make very much eye contact with him, for he was too consumed in his truck to be available for that.

Another little piece of divinity, perhaps...

"Word gets around." He glanced at me. Winked at me. The two of us smiled. "So what are you gonna do with her?" he asked, looking back at his work.

He was under his truck now.

"Do with her? Like how?"

"Take her to the prom? I don't know..."

I laughed. "Maybe. The thing is..."

I figured I might as well go for it...

"...because of my situation, I don't know how...romantic this can get."

I sensed him nodding, even though I couldn't see him. What he said to me next proved really important:

"Just remember, kid: Romance is 99 percent in the mind."

"How's that?"

"Think of it this way: You got plenty of pretty girls in your school, right?"

"I'm still with the tutor."

"Yeah, but you'll go back. Pretty girls there, right?"

"Of course."

"So before I asked your grandma to marry me, there was this other girl, about as beautiful as Grandma, who I was maybe also seeing from time to time..."

I laughed silently. What was Angus, a secret ladies man??

"I was 19, which for your generation is still young, but for mine was about time to settle down. So I knew it was between your grandma and this other lady, Victoria. And Victoria was very beautiful. And charming, too. The fellas I hung around with were all jealous. But I'll tell you what, Tucker:

"Victoria was a witch."

I smiled. "Like how?"

"Oh, many ways. She could be hostile. She'd snap at you. Your grandmother was nothing like that: She was always very kind. Now, in a way, Victoria offered more excitement, 'cause she was unpredictable. But I didn't need to spend my life dealing with that. So the choice was easy. Do you see my point?"

"I...think so?"

He rolled out toward me from under the truck. Our faces were in diagonal alignment. He was about three feet away, in crisp, perfect focus.

"The outer package means nothing. It's the soul that matters."

"Yeah..." I kind of rolled my eyes. "I get that. But my outer package has major limits."

"Tucker..."

"Yeah?"

"Look at me."

So I did. His eyes bore infinite depth.

"The outer package," he said again, "means noth-ing."

* * *

It took a month before we took things further.

First few times, it was on the floor. A few encounters in a row, she kissed me before it was time for me to leave. She couldn't do it in front of our parents, so she kept an eye on the clock, then leaned over and did it, like, two minutes before my dad was set to show. I liked the pattern, but I wanted more.

Around the 30-day mark, after we'd hung out a good dozen times, our conversations kept creeping back to the idea that we were "best friends." But then there was of course the kissing. That left me a little in between worlds. She was sending mixed messages.

"That's what girls do," said Jordan, as he drove me to her place one day.

"But why?" I wasn't complaining; I was actually curious. Where did that get them? It seemed to just keep everything muddled.

As Jordan spoke, he moved his fingers the way an orchestra conductor moves his baton, sort of tracking the rhythms of his words, the ups and downs: "They're poking around, you see. They're dropping hints. But it's not committal. They're waiting on you for that part."

"But she kisses me."

"You told me that."

"At least once every time."

"Like...friend kisses?"

"No, not like 'friend' kisses. She lets them last."

"Tongue?"

"A little. Sometimes."

"A little? Now *you're* sending mixed messages,

bro..."

I smiled. I thought about it. At least twice, she'd been assertive with her tongue. It was a little surreal when it happened, and definitely on the speedy side, to the point where I had to mentally replay it to remind myself that it was real.

But it was.

In addition, she'd had, like, mints or something the past few times. Or at least brushed her teeth in advance. Her mouth was fresh. She'd been preparing for the action, thinking it over ahead of time.

"No," I said, "she gives me her tongue."

"Okay, so...you're in. She wouldn't be seeing you like every two seconds if you weren't."

"But she calls me her 'best friend'. What's that about?"

"Ah..." Jordan closed his mouth and squinted ahead, thinking over the implications.

"What?" I asked him.

He kept on squinting.

"Have I been friend-zoned?" I was starting to slip back into panic mode. For a while now, I'd been leaning toward a cooler place, one wherein confidence shaded my being. Every once in a while, though, I was back there in Colsen, in that bed, my mind buzzing and chattering with all the many angles and possibilities regarding Rebecca.

"No," said Jordan. "Not friend-zoned. That's ridiculous."

"Why?"

"Because the 'zone' is an actual zone, with borders around it. You get put there, you know it. Her body's off limits."

"So what's she doing then? That's a mixed message, right?"

"Correct. And a test."

"What's the test?"

"She says 'best friend' again: You call her out. You ask her what that means. Show her you care."

I looked out the window. All those houses going by. So much life behind those doors, walls, and windows. So many dramas unfolding, all over the world. Love, hate, hope, fear.

And here was me, in the midst of it all, looking to outsiders like the guy at the bottom, the guy whom everybody else is most afraid of becoming. But not a single one of them could get me. They couldn't get that I wanted exactly what almost all of them wanted. I wasn't some freak, broken on the inside.

On the contrary, my interior world was more bright and fiery than ever before. To a large extent, it was all I had. So I wasn't about to let it fall to neglect, not keeping the plants watered and the carpets shampooed. No, I had to be an able housekeeper.

If only they knew.

If only they knew I was just like them.

If only they knew all I wanted in this world was to be loved.

* * *

But I wasn't about to go all mushy on her.

I waited, though, as we chatted. My ears were on high alert. I wasn't going to be too eager and visit the topic without being prompted, but just the same, I wasn't going to let it slide when it finally came.

And come it did. While she was on the phone.

Her friend "Becky" called. Becky was actually called Rebecca at school, but since she shared a name with "my" Rebecca, she got tagged Becky when the two of them spoke. They weren't too-too close, but they hung out every now and again. They were applying to some of the same colleges, which meant there was an outside chance they'd end up at the same one together, so a little preparatory bonding was called for, just in case.

"I gotta go," said Rebecca, after they chatted about homework and talked smack about a teacher for less than five minutes. "I'm here with my best friend."

She hung up.

I looked at her. I was on the couch across from her bed. I knew and she knew that my look wasn't the warmest one in the world. For she'd not only ventured into the controversial wording, but she'd done so with a third party.

I didn't like that. Felt very alone about it, in fact.

And mad.

I launched right into my objection. Granted, I

knew I had a lot to lose. I didn't want to be the handicapped kid causing drama from his chair, forcing his
friends and loved ones to wheel him into the corner
where he could never be heard from again. On the
other hand, what was I, her little prop? Her practice
doll?

I was seething. She saw it. And I was glad, because
I wasn't about to hide it.

"Why do you call me that?"

"Call you what?"

I didn't even have to speak again.

She shrugged. "My mom..."

"You weren't talking to your mom."

"I know. But that's what my mom thinks, so I keep
it that way."

"But you say it to me, too."

"But it's true!"

Her face was getting pink. She didn't seem embarrassed, exactly, although I'd definitely succeeded in
making her uncomfortable, which was fine by me – for
the time being.

"But, like, what am I, really? First you say it's just
a thing you say to your mom, which makes me feel like
it's not really true. Then you say it to Becky, and – like
– why would *Becky* care either way?"

"Tucker: It just came out that way. I was just talking."

"Fine. Then that sounds like it wasn't what you
meant."

"I guess not." She looked away, toward the mess of colorful posters on her wall. When she finally looked back, her eyes were shining. Moisture. "What do you want to be the case?" she asked.

There it was. My opening. Nice and wide. I wasn't about to use words like "boyfriend" and "girlfriend", but I certainly wasn't about to let this "friend" stuff stand.

"Together," I said. "I want to be with you."

"You do?" A tear slid down her cheek.

"Of course," I had to clinch my vocal cords a touch to avoid reaching too high a pitch. "What else are we doing here?"

"Hanging out, I thought."

"But other stuff..."

We looked at each other. She wiped her cheek with the end of her sleeve. Our silence seemed to fill the room. Just when I thought it would finally end, it swung back around for a couple more laps.

I remembered what Jordan had said: that girls sent mixed messages 'cause they wanted us to be the ones to clarify things. So as much as I wanted her to be the one to break the silence, I decided to stay on my assertive tract:

"Why would you even think for a second that I didn't want that?" I asked her.

She shrugged. "I don't know. You're going through something."

I could tell, right then, that she didn't want to cry,

but she did. It was audible. Were her mom in the hall-way, she would have overheard. Everything in my be-ing wanted to get up and go to her, to hold her, to stroke her back, to tell her to let it all out.

But I couldn't.

So instead I said, "I'm not 'going through' any-thing, Rebecca. I'm in it. I'm in this, now. This is me."

"I know," she said, and the words were laced with a great, true sadness. "And..." She gave me her eyes as she said this. "...I don't always know how to be or what to do."

That was it for me. I started to cry, as well. The tears sneaked up on me. I'd cried before in front of peo-ple I was close to, but never a girl, and never this soon.

And certainly never during this kind of a discus-sion.

"I don't know how to be, either," I said, having trouble forming the words. The strange thing was, the words weren't altogether true. Somehow, I'd known exactly how to be. One word held my mandate to-gether:

Strength.

That was all I knew. So I wondered for a second there if I was manipulating her – just mirroring her statement and her emotion so she'd like me more, or something.

Just so we could be...together.

Then again, maybe my words were true, after all. True enough, anyway. 'Cause what did I really know about anything? I was certainly up against something heavy here. Dwelling on it did me no good, so I'd made a habit of dwelling on her.

When I looked my paralysis in the eye – when I combed back all my other thoughts and gave it a good, clean, naked stare – it had a way of turning my core to ice.

So...yeah...I was being sincere. I went on to say, "I'm just getting through it. And I'm happy to have you to get through it with."

I wiped my own tears away with my hooked hand.

The next thing I knew, she was on me, kissing me. I touched her back...her front. She kissed my neck. So soft.

My world lit up.

Together, on that day, we spent time on the couch for a good couple hours.

* * *

"How experienced are you?" I asked her.

This was just past the one-month mark, around our third session of more or less making out.

I didn't just blurt it out. It had come in context. She'd been asking me if I liked the way she kissed my neck. She explained to me that she'd read in a book about sex that it's less awkward to ask your partner about his or her preferences than to just try and wing it. Winging it creates too much awkwardness. Open communication, Rebecca explained, is the key to romantic satisfaction.

That was fine by me. My verbal faculty was a much-valued tool. In this particular instance, I used it to ask, "You're reading a book about sex?"

She nodded.

And then: "How experienced are you?"

"Like...not."

"Huh?" My eyebrows ascended.

"Not at all, really." She shrugged with one shoulder, kept it raised for a moment. It was definitely awkward. I looked at the shoulder and we both laughed. "How 'bout you?"

"I don't know. Like, third base. A little beyond, maybe..."

"Maybe...?"

I smiled, doing my own version of a shrug, which I managed to evoke through my facial muscles. "Not all the way," I said, clarifying things in terms of the big question.

"But you can." She formed the words as a statement, but I sensed the ghost of a question mark hanging in the air right after them. We'd visited this topic before, of course, and I wasn't about to change my answer.

"Yeah." It came out quietly, borderline inaudible. But she heard it, and nodded, and before I knew it we were kissing again...

AUSTIN CHARTERS

* * *

I started hanging out with a new group of guys, also.

Double Mike was by now ancient history. At first, his sudden absence had burned me, but now that I had a good thing going with Rebecca, as far as I was concerned I was beyond his realm. He would have been so envious had he still been my friend. I privately hoped that word about me and Rebecca would float its way over to him, but even if it didn't – whatever. I still had her, and knew how beautiful she was, and that was enough.

This new crowd was different. They weren't quite as "cool", at least not in the old-school sense. See, there's classic cool and there's what I think of as new cool. Classic cool is James Dean. Classic cool is cigarettes and angst and being a badass. New cool, however, is something different. It's less of an outward style, and more about just being who you are. New cool's more all-encompassing and accepting than classic cool. A geek can have new-coolness. A shy person can be new-cool. It's not really specific, so long as you keep it real.

I guess what I'm trying to say is, from the outside, this gang would have seemed a little geeky. I met them at the library, of all places. My mom (and dad, but really my mom) thought it'd be a good idea for me to join a club, since I wasn't due to stop the tutoring 'til after winter break. That meant about two more months of alternating between home and Rebecca's place, with Rebecca making the occasional trip to my place (a situation I tried to avoid, actually, 'cause in spite of it being more logistically convenient for me, it opened up the possibility of my dad paying too close attention).

One day my mom opened a booklet in front of me on the kitchen table.

"What's this?"

"The clubs. The library. I told you."

I sighed. We'd discussed it once, and I was half-hoping it would never come up again. But now with the booklet right there in front of me, I got a gander at all my wondrous and delightful (note my sarcasm) social options.

Movie clubs. Book clubs. Game clubs. Drama clubs. It was actually a little mystifying to me that people actually did this stuff. It seemed so innocent in a way. Did any of them realize how corny they were behaving, or were they simply too busy enjoying themselves?

I kind of wished my mom had instead put a booklet of support groups in front of me. Maybe I could chat with some other people in my position. Then again, my mom was probably too smart for that, as it opened up the serious possibility of me getting depressed. She knew I was still a kid, and that kids do best when among other kids.

I decided to be a good sport and join the movie club.

It was kind of fun, actually. On my first outing there, as much as I wanted to disappear down a hole and hide forever, I was a little relieved to find out that there wasn't always that much talk about movies. I mean, every time we got together, we watched a movie, but that didn't mean we were forced to talk about it before and after. Sometimes we did, sometimes we didn't. It was never forced. If we didn't talk about the movie, we got into more social stuff, which basically meant making stupid and/or crazy jokes about ourselves or the other people at the library.

One time the flick we watched was the original "Die Hard", and that got a decent conversation going. Everybody thought it was really intense. We all agreed that the main character, John McClane, had kept pushing forward where most guys would have backed down.

I liked that. It spoke to me. Even though it was a violent and bloody movie, it was kind of inspiring in that sense.

It was about a hero.

And I used our conversation about it to segway into some discussion about Rebecca...

* * *

To me, it made sense. By pursuing Rebecca, I was being Bruce Willis. I didn't have any statistics on the topic, but I was pretty sure most guys in my position weren't being actively romantic. Tony had once mentioned a paralyzed guy he knew hiring a prostitute, which was certainly something I had no interest in ever exploring. In a way, I was lucky that Rebecca had been assertive at just the right time, but my ego couldn't give luck all the credit. I had to also give myself points for being desirable; otherwise I was just some passive dude letting life roll over him.

I didn't tell the movie club guys that I was Bruce Willis in my own head, 'cause that would have lost me their friendship pretty quick, but I did tell them that I thought there was the possibility of something serious happening.

"Like, how serious?" my bro Anthony asked.

"All the way?" Tim chimed in.

"All the way," I confirmed, nodding with my eyes.

"Can you do that?" Anthony asked.

"Dude!" This was Alex speaking: the voice of reason.

"No, it's okay," I said, saving Alex from a moralistic speech.

Alex nodded. I looked back at Anthony: "I can do it," I said. "But I'm not a hundred percent sure."

"So what's 'I can do it' mean?" Anthony wanted to know.

"Means my body gets going sometimes on its own, like when I'm sleeping, but I haven't ever tested it out with a girl."

They all sat silently for a moment. I briefly worried

they'd get awkward and betray me by bringing up a safer topic. But as it turned out, they were grateful for the chance to talk about something exciting:

"Then you'll be fine," Anthony assured me.

"How do you know?" I asked.

He shrugged. "If your body works then your body works."

"But she's gotta be on top," said Alex.

"What does he care?" asked Tim. "That's good news!"

They all laughed. Yet I didn't. I found myself feeling a little vulnerable. Not even Jordan knew about my concern in this regard.

"When will you try?" asked Anthony.

"Soon, I hope."

"Like next time you see her?"

"Probably not."

"Then when."

"I don't know. She says--"

* * *

"I want to go slow."

Her words were filled with breath. We were on her couch again. Our session had gone pretty far: her shirt was off, and her eyes kept flicking toward the (locked) door.

"Okay," I said, also breathing hard.

My body hadn't been triggered by the session, but

I sensed (hoped) it could have been if we'd lasted just a few more minutes.

To be honest, I was a little disappointed to see her stop, if only because I was in so much suspense as to how things would go down there.

"You know I care about you," I said, running my knuckles along the top of her arm.

"I know. Of course." She smiled.

"So we go when you're ready."

She didn't answer that. She didn't seem upset, just somehow less than present. As her breath cooled down, she got dressed again. We listened to the music playing on her computer. Casually, she reached over and unlocked the door – signaling to me, I think, that she wasn't going to revisit that territory again today.

I got the message. Along with another one:

She hadn't answered me when I said, "when you're ready." That meant it wasn't a definite "when." It was an "if."

My facial muscles grew tense.

This wasn't a done deal, I realized then. Christmas break was right around the corner, which meant my family would be spending a week in San Diego. I had no clue how I'd deal with a week without Rebecca.

And I was pretty determined to take things further with her before we left...

* * *

"Where's Dad?"

I was frantic. Trying to hold it in, but "it" was pretty massive, and was leaking out all over the place, in the form of steam from my ears and laser beams from my eyes.

"Don't know." Jordan headed toward the door, taking a bite from a salami sandwich in the process.

"What do you mean? He's supposed to drive me."

Jordan shrugged, in a world of his own. "Shopping, I think."

I wheeled my chair toward the front door, almost banging into Jordan's heels. "For what??"

For the first time in this rather tense (at least for me) exchange, Jordan turned to face me. 'Til then, it was almost like he hadn't known I was there. "I don't know," he said, his words dripping with agitation. "Call him. Ask him. Stuff for our trip, I think."

Come Sunday morning, we were headed to San Diego. One whole week. It was awful timing: Christmas Break. Rebecca would be home all day, every day, yet I'd be suffering through tourist stops and stranger stares with my family.

Right now it was Friday afternoon, and I *had to* get to Rebecca's house. I was running out of days.

"Can you take me?" I asked Jordan.

He sneered. This wasn't, like, the week after my accident. Almost four months had gone by. Everybody was getting more used to the state of things. In other words, Jordan wasn't about to go getting all sympathetic on me:

"No," he said, the word hard and flat. "I'm busy."

"Come on! It's easy for you!"

"It's not. We gotta get you in the car, we gotta get you out--"

"Oh, real tough life you have. Where are you even going?"

"Date. Later."

Jordan was gone.

I couldn't remember ever having been so furious. My dad was supposed to take me at four, and it was now almost a quarter to five. My mom was at her sister's place, and I was pretty sure that "shopping", however much Jordan had believed it, was just another word for "drinking."

As Jordan pulled away, a second strike against my dad emerged: I was now home alone. Jordan certainly didn't seem to care, let alone my dad, and as grateful as I was to be entrusted to look after myself, the fact of the matter was, I was being forgotten about.

And a paralyzed person home alone is pretty much an emergency waiting to happen.

I rolled over to the kitchen table, where my cell phone awaited. Its battery was on the brink of dead. I navigated to my dad's number and dialed.

Three rings. Each one seemed to take longer than the last...

"'Ello?"

"Dad! Where are you? I'm waiting!"

"Waiting for what, Tucker?"

"To go to Rebecca's. You said!"

A pause here. I half-expected him to hang up. But instead, he did something arguably worse. He said, "Can't do it, kid. I'm in no condition to drive."

"What does that mean??"

Then he hung up.

* * *

Fortunately, my mom was on my side. When I told her what my dad had said, she started barking about what a jerk he was. Then she said she'd come home within the hour.

It was just past five now. No good. Rebecca only had 'til seven, then her family had some dinner thing. It wasn't enough time.

"Can you come sooner?" I asked.

"Sit tight," my mom said.

"Yeah, that's all I *can* do."

I hung up. Looked around, thinking. The movie group guys were all sophomores and juniors. A couple of them could drive, but this was a pretty big – and potentially – annoying favor, asking them to come pick me up from my house and drop me off at somebody else's, with the potential need to come back and get me again later, and to top it all off, no invitation to join me in hanging out with Rebecca.

It would be selfish. It would be unforgivable.

It was my only option.

I dialed Anthony and told him what was what. Since he'd been sympathetic to my plight from the first time I mentioned having sex with Rebecca, I figured maybe he'd help a brother out.

He hesitated, however. "My dad might have to come," he said.

"Why?" I felt my breath getting clenched.

"I just got my license. I don't always get to drive alone."

"You come alone to the library."

"Yeah, but that's an easy route."

My blood boiled. "Fine, um...can your dad come?"

"I have to call you back."

"Okay."

"What's your address?"

My heart leaped. Excitement. "562," I started.

Then my phone died.

* * *

"NOOOOOOOOOO!!!"

That wasn't what I screamed when my phone went dead.

It was what I screamed when I realized that the charger was upstairs. We had one downstairs, in the kitchen, but it was broken. Everybody kept saying we needed to go get a new one, but nobody ever did anything about it.

I of course blamed this oversight on the rest of my family, seeing as I was limited in terms of procuring solutions, to say the least.

In a meager, pathetic stab at hope – with no shortage of straining and struggling and swearing – I managed to plug my dead phone in atop the kitchen counter with the bad charger. Nope: God wasn't about to grace me with a sudden miracle. The phone was still dead, and now attached to a dead charger for good measure.

I tried to slow my mind down. I thought of God for a bit. I recalled everything I'd heard at church about lust. I was being too eager, but it wasn't altogether my fault. My dad had *promised* to take me there. So I wasn't so much reacting to my inability to see Rebecca as my dad's broken promise.

Meanwhile, why hadn't Rebecca called?

The more I wondered about that one, the more hurt and achy I became inside. Granted, I'd never failed to show up before, so she had every reason to think I'd be there at any moment, but still: I'd been running over half an hour late by the time my phone died. Wasn't that beyond a normal window? Shouldn't she have tried me after 10 minutes?

Did she even care? Did *anybody* care about me?

After 20 minutes or so, my mom came home, holding two hot bags stuffed with fried chicken she'd grabbed from a drive-thru. I was grateful for the chicken – to say nothing of the company – but I was less than understanding when she told me she couldn't take me to Rebecca's.

"Why?" I asked.

"Because honey, we have to go and get your dad."

"No."

"Tucker..."

"*What?*" By now, I was averting my eyes. "I'll just stay here," I muttered.

"You *can't* stay here."

I looked at her, lancing her with my gaze. "Why not? Everybody left me here. Dad's in a gutter--"

"Tucker!"

"--Jordan walked out and hardly looked at me. Let me just stay home. I'm in a bad mood."

"We both know that's a bad idea. Come on. We'll get your dad and you can give him a piece of your mind."

I eyed her anew, collecting my breath.

That sounded good and awful at the same time.

* * *

In the end, as it turned out, God was on my side.

Never before had I seen my dad drunk. I mean, I was pretty sure I *had* at some point or another, but never before had it been this overt.

I was waiting on the little sidewalk path outside a bar called Half Nelson's when my mom walked him outside. She hadn't had to make any other stops; somehow or another, she knew this was his place. The bar's name struck me as lame and irrelevant. Wasn't that a wrestling move or something? Anyway, I guess it didn't matter, so long as the patrons kept on coming back to buy more booze.

When you sell something addictive, marketing becomes something of an afterthought.

Even the sign on the door seemed to be on its way out – to say nothing of the big-bellied people I saw drifting in and out the door. Hunched shoulders. Perpetually squinting eyes. Sitting there, I wondered if I wasn't in fact the lucky one. I mean, there I was with a broken neck, and determined to make the most of my life, and here were these people, with their bodies fully intact and operational (more or less), letting everything slip away to the bottom of a bottle.

Without a doubt, they had their own problems. Everyone did; that's a fact of life. So I felt a little bad for judging them. Just the same, however, I myself was the certified owner of a pretty bad problem. So although sitting in judgment isn't healthy for any soul, I found myself feeling bad for these people.

So much potential.

So much waste.

And here came one such person right now...

My mom wasn't holding my dad by the arm or anything, but she may as well have been. He looked like the ashamed pupil walking alongside the angry principal. It would have been comical were it not so sad.

ROLLING HOME

By then, I was pretty pissed off – beyond furious. The sun had gone down; the sky was pitch black. And beyond my own urgency to get to Rebecca – or at least return home to my charged phone and see if she'd called – I was starting to realize in a deep way that my dad had a problem. It wasn't just a pity for his family, and it was certainly more than an inconvenience.

The guy was suffering.

Though like those of his bar-mates, his problem seemed, through my eyes, to be of relatively manageable proportions.

Then again, he had to be carrying a pretty big dragon on his back to flake out on his son for the sake of drinking. I knew he loved me. I could feel it. Despite the tension that hung in the air between us, despite the way my nerves buckled when he so much as made eye contact with me, I knew he was a good enough guy to want to do better than disappoint me.

Much less my mom. Or Jordan.

As for Grandpa – oh man, don't even get me started. How shameful would that be, for Grandpa Angus to find out that his daughter had married a drunk? And how ironic that situation would be, in light of all Grandpa Angus himself had to be ashamed about...

My dad shot me a look.

He wasn't defiant. Was far from strong.

He, like me, was fully ashamed.

I broke the eye contact.

The two of them walked past me to the car.

* * *

It was in the backseat that I hatched my plan.

My dad rode shotgun while my mom drove, of course. His head was buried in his headrest, and his eyes were closed but his eyeballs were stirring like two dots of frying bacon.

He wasn't sleeping, that much was clear.

He just likely wanted to avoid my mother's wrath.

"I want to go to Rebecca's," I said.

"Tucker..." my mom started.

But I cut her off: "This is too sad. Please – just let me spend the night."

I saw my mom's eyes, sad to the point of nearly bursting, studying me in the rear-view mirror. It was true, what I'd said, but a ploy nonetheless.

On the one hand, being around my dad while he was drunk was torture.

On the other hand, I was just looking for a way to see my girlfriend.

My mom's not stupid; she more than likely saw through the whole thing. At the same time, she probably did deem it a good idea.

And probably wanted the space to give my dad a good old-fashioned piece of her mind.

"Will her parents be OK with that?"

"I think so. That one time I fell asleep there."

I was referring to an incident from about 10 days prior. It wasn't that I'd fallen asleep – it was that my dad had been about five hours late to pick me up. When he pulled up the driveway after 1AM, Rebecca's parents were more than friendly, acting like they thought him appearing so late made for perfectly normal and civilized behavior, but anyone who wasn't blind could see the tension winding its way right up their spines.

When I got in the car that night, I pretended to sleep the whole ride home.

Just like he was doing right now...

Only in my case, I didn't keep my eyes closed to avoid a confrontation; I kept them closed because I was worried he'd get us into a fatal accident.

And I'd already had more accidents than I could handle.

* * *

"Call if you need me," my mom whispered on Rebecca's porch.

She gave me a kiss on the cheek. It was cold, though. Not on account of her feelings toward me – which I'd always been able to depend on being warm – but because she was so knocked over by my dad's behavior.

Then just like that, she was gone.

And Rebecca was standing over me, and smiling.

"I thought you'd never make it," she said, curling around me so as to wheel me into her house.

"Me neither," I said. "Long story."

We got inside. Hit a couple of bumps in the process, but that was to be expected in homes that weren't wheelchair-ready. By now, I had memorized the Rebecca-house bumps. And she had gotten really good at taking care of me, to the point where everyone in my family knew I was entirely okay being alone with her (to the point where I was safe spending the night). Meanwhile, through some form of divine intervention, the doorways in her home were pretty wide. Not perfect, but good enough to grant me reasonable freedom of motion.

Which, in turn, led to other forms of freedom...

* * *

It took me a while to relax that night.

When I found myself surrounded by the familiar sights and scents of Rebecca's bedroom – so girly, so pink, so filled with stuffed animals, and yet so second nature to me by now – I kind of expected to come down from the adrenaline of my whole evening, but in actuality it started to seem like the walls were closing in on me.

"What happened?"

She plopped herself down on her mattress, causing some of her ever-staring stuffed animals to hop and land.

If I were able to shrug, that would have been the

most appropriate reply.

Should I open up to her? About my dad?

Gosh, the last thing I wanted was to become a "problem" guy. Trapped in a wheelchair. Alcoholic father. Next thing I knew, she'd be keeping her distance.

But the truth was the truth, and particularly after that incident from 10 days prior, there was really no use in keeping it hidden.

"I think my dad's got a thing for the bottle."

She made soft eye contact with me. "Yeah," she said.

Clear as day: She knew already.

Which meant her parents knew, as well.

Either she'd smelled it or seen it, or maybe heard it from somewhere else.

Funny how when you grant a voice to something that's been hidden, the reaction's usually not as extreme as you expected it to be. Despite all their blind spots and distractions, people tend to know what's going on. Maybe they don't exactly rush to talk about it, but when you go first, they're often not sluggish when it comes to following.

"Is it bad?" she asked.

I shrugged with my lower lip. "Don't know," I said.

But I thought it was. Or getting bad. Or at least approaching the point where he was unable to keep it under wraps.

And if the way I felt was any measure, then this

was a pretty shitty situation, indeed.

Rebecca knew that; it was in her eyes. Her eyes, which stayed on me as she rose from the bed.

Her eyes, which soaked me up as she moved closer to me...

And as she helped me move out of my chair and onto her bed.

* * *

"Are we finally gonna do it?" I asked.

The two of us laughed. I just had to throw the word "finally" in there, didn't I? I felt justified in doing so, though, not only because we'd waited a while, but because...yes...oh, man...

Something was stirring down there.

She touched me in between my legs.

I couldn't feel it...but I knew.

I was there. It was happening down there...

She looked from my pants to my eyes. "Okay," she said.

My blood started moving through my veins like cars around a raceway track...

Things went a little fast after that. Or I should say: Rebecca made things move a little fast. After all, she was the one doing almost all the moving.

She unzipped me. She slid my jeans off. Then my boxers.

Then that was it: She saw.

I saw, too.

Though I couldn't see it all. I had to prop my head up as best I could. It was there, though, in plain sight.

And then it wasn't.

'Cause Rebecca had climbed on top of me. On top of it. And around it.

I went inside of her.

Yet still, she didn't slip down all the way. She was perched a little. Her knees weren't level: one was on the mattress, the other was bent up.

"What's wrong?" I asked.

"It's just..." She breathed. Her teeth were clenched. "First time..."

"It's okay," I said.

"It hurts a little."

"I know. Go slow."

She did. But it was still too fast, and she hissed out breath. "I need a second," she said.

My eyes darted about. The word "condom" flashed inside my head, but I knew that wasn't what she meant. I mean, it's not exactly like I was sleeping with every girl in the neighborhood...

She was gone for a moment. I looked at her body. My head was out swimming. Heart was throbbing. I wanted her back in that bed.

It didn't happen right away, but more than a minute later, she was back. Squatting beside me. Touching herself down there.

My head snapped down against the mattress. I

was getting a little tired keeping it propped up. I sucked some air in.

This was it.

This *had* to be it...

She was back on top of me again. I put my hands on each of her hips, then slid them down the soft skin to her thighs.

Held her.

Her knees went level this time.

She was doing it...

We were doing it...

...and then we weren't.

* * *

Story of my life.

I lay there wondering whether or not it had happened. If it had, it had only been for 60 – maybe 90 – seconds at most. But something thick was in the air.

Something told me this waiting wasn't over yet.

She snuggled up close to me. After a few stale, eternal moments, she whispered, "We'll try again later."

"Okay," I said.

I gave her a smile.

A true smile, at that. I was crazy about her. We lay together with my right arm wrapped around her. Her shirt and bra were still on, but nothing else. I felt so close to her at that moment. Closer than I'd ever felt to anyone before.

Yet still, deep inside, was this gnawing fear...

What if I just couldn't get there next time?

I felt dumb for having such a thought. In fact, my body's ability to get there had been as pleasant a surprise as Angus's bullet coming from that gun had been an unpleasant one.

Just the same, the ground beneath me felt so soft at times...

My mood got slippery. Before I knew it, it went gray. Not black...more of a twilight shade. I rubbed her back and thought of my dad. The whole damn evening. The fact that I was in this bed now 'cause I'd played a hand against his drunkenness.

Which one of my parents had that in their genes? The ability to angle and manipulate?

It was far from my proudest trait, for sure. Be that as it may, I blamed my dad for it. It was he, after all, who was always out for hours at a stretch: destination unknown. It was he who struggled through conversations wherein his breath smelled just a few notches too severe for waking daylight.

He who walked around filled up with pain.

But why? What was wrong with him?

What happens to a guy to make him like that?

* * *

In my dream, I wasn't falling, exactly...

But the entire room around me was.

I was in the kitchen with my mother. Our house was falling, for some strange reason. Down an infinite rabbit hole.

No bottom in sight.

No bottom even worth *imagining...*

My mom spoke words to me, but I had trouble hearing. At the same time, though, I absorbed their meaning.

We were undergoing a kind of storm.

I'd never heard of such a storm before, but – *whoa!* – was this house *falling* or what? It was INSANE! Some unknowable breed of gravity was yanking us down, down, down, down...

Yet my mother seemed calm. She held the counter. Tense inside – I could spy that in her gaze – but composed overall.

Then a terrifying thought occurred to me:

"When will we ever get back?" I asked.

She looked at me.

But she wasn't my mom anymore.

She was an upright goat: head of a goat, body of a gray-haired human.

"We will not," uttered the goat.

* * *

I woke up beside Rebecca, drenched in sweat.

It took me a second to remember that we were both half-naked. Then I got worried that the door wasn't locked. Her poor parents – they no doubt thought I wasn't capable of being "romantic" with their daughter.

A model of respectability.

Here in her bedroom, helping her bid farewell to her innocence.

"You're heart's beating fast," she said.

Her hand was under my shirt, on my chest. The sound of her voice sneaked up on me. If I wasn't mistaken, my sweat increased.

"Had a bad dream," I said.

She moved in closer. Both our bodies: sealed together.

"What was it?" she asked.

I explained it to her. Every detail. I thought she might laugh when I mentioned the goat, but it seemed to scare her almost as much as it had scared me.

"What do you think it means?" she asked.

"I was gonna ask *you* that," I said.

She thought about it. So much darkness in her room. So perfect, in a way, what with the mystery it offered. We could be anywhere, the two of us.

Anyone, in fact.

I couldn't even see my chair (though if I squinted, I could make out its wheels' silver shine...).

"I think it means," she said, sitting up on one elbow, "uncertainty. Falling. Nothing underneath."

"Like me," I said.

"Huh?"

I looked at her. Her face was right there, but I could only make out its broadest outlines. "Like me," I repeated.

And the second time, my voice cracked.

Great. Was I about to cry?

I didn't. That little burst of emotion had been the extent of what that moment had in store.

"You're there," she said, her hand drifting downward, tracing the length of my side, stomach, thigh...

"You're right here," she whispered to me in the dark.

"I know," I said, attempting a smile.

Could she see it? Could she sense it?

"You're ready again," she reported.

I propped my head up, then looked to my left. The alarm clock provided the room's only light. Lime green numbers.

It was half past four.

As for the lower half of my body, that was well beyond my sight.

"Do you want to?" I asked.

But I didn't have to.

She wasn't next to me anymore. She was upright, walking two steps on her knees.

I waited. She went upward, and downward, knees aligned.

On me.

Around me...

A click occurred. I couldn't feel it with my body,

but I sensed it from the way she moved. The way her breath escaped her. She'd crossed the barrier.

I was up inside.

She moved, then. Back and forth, a little.

Front to back.

The darkness grew lesser.

And she made sounds.

As before, I reached up, held her waist. Such soft skin. Such a beautiful girl.

It lasted this time for a good long while. She was the one who decided to make it last. I, in fact, drifted into confusion at times:

Was it over yet? Did more remain?

Usually the answer was the latter.

Until it wasn't anymore.

Until she was back beside me again, this time producing a lot of breath, with a heartbeat so rapid that I imagined I could feel her pulse by way of my fingertips, as I traced them along her legs.

"That was nice," she said.

I smiled, breathless.

She came forward and kissed me on the cheek. Then the mouth.

Then we held each other 'til the light came through the window and the day began.

CHAPTER 6

Turning

We did it one more time before I had to leave.

So it was twice altogether, or two and a half if you want to get picky about it. The final time was the best, however, as I asked her to kiss my neck and ears, just as she had in the weeks leading up to this weekend, when we'd been making out. For me, any kind of soft touch from her on those parts of my body gave me the equivalent of what I imagined an orgasm would be. Of course, I couldn't know what a real one felt like, but I figured somewhere in the lowermost reaches of my mind, that information was there. Kind of like human beings are computers: Even when you're not running a particular program, the knowledge on how to use it is packed away deep in the hardware.

I figured my approximation of an orgasm had to be pretty close to the real thing.

And whether I was right or wrong, I figured it'd be a good idea to see Rebecca again as soon as possible.

* * *

Just the same, we had kind of a rapid goodbye that morning. Everything came together to get me out of the house fast. First, my mom called and said it'd be a good idea for her to come and get me, so I could get packed for our trip the next day. Then Rebecca's mom knocked on her door kind of loud, and when Rebecca answered I overheard a lot of hurried whispering.

Rebecca didn't have to tell me what was up:

We'd obviously crossed something of a line with me staying all night.

It wasn't a big deal. Rebecca didn't seem up in arms about it. As before, her parents couldn't possibly imagine what we had been up to. And even if they had, they had to presume that my limitations made for a limited amount of scandal.

Or so I hoped.

In the meantime, I was even picking up the vibe from Rebecca that I should get going. Even though I'd be gone for a whole week, there didn't seem to be any energy pushing toward the option of us spending the day together.

This made me sad...for about half a second.

Truth was, I needed to get home and to my own room – and fast. I wanted to just be in my own bed, catching up on the sleep I'd missed in her room, and giving myself the chance to process what had happened.

On the whole, it was such a giant deal, and yet in those moments before I left her house, it all seemed so tiny and ordinary.

We sat at the kitchen table eating waffles, and Rebecca chatted with her mom about boring things while I waited for my own mom to show:

"Tucker's going to San Diego," said Rebecca.

"Oh yeah?" said her mom, not even turning from the counter to face me, so glued were her eyes to the coupon book laid out before her. "What's in San Diego?"

"I don't know," I said. "Just...shopping. The zoo. See some relatives."

"Well, that sounds nice."

Ordinarily, I would have said something polite. Probably agreed with the grown-up's assessment. But at that moment, no – it didn't sound nice at all. No, nice would have been coming right back to this place.

Seeing Rebecca.

Having more of what we'd had.

* * *

When she said goodbye to me before helping me into my mom's car, I should have guessed right then and there that something was up:

"Have a good trip," she said.

"I will. I'll call you."

"Okay."

She leaned over and kissed my cheek.

I smiled, but I couldn't really see her since the sun was positioned right behind her in the sky. And truth be told, I didn't really see her again – not in the vivid sense – until after I got back from my trip.

In the weeks to come, that little moment with Rebecca being washed out by sunlight would come to symbolize what had happened to us the night before.

* * *

"Do you love Dad?"

I swear my mom almost swerved into a tree. But the truth was, the question came from a place of sincerity.

"Tucker!"

"I'm serious."

"How could you ask me that? Of course I do!"

"Don't just say it 'cause I'm your kid – and his. I've been through a lot."

"What's that mean?"

"It means I know things. I can see."

"And you think you see that I don't love your

dad??"

"No!" I smiled. "But I can see how it works between human beings. You disappoint each other. Sometimes we let each other down, and though we love the person, deep inside, it's hard to mend what's been broken."

My mom's brows lowered, nearly touching each other, as she processed this sudden commentary on human relationships.

"Is this really about me and your dad?"

Uh-oh...She'd found me out...

"Or is this about you and that girl?"

I aimed my eyes out the window. All those lives going on out there. All the drama. How many people had had sex the night before? If you considered how many babies found their way into the world, it had to be a whole hell of a lot...

I tried to answer my mom's question in my head, but nothing was coming together in a concrete way. Yeah, I felt weird about Rebecca. Or not...weird, exactly. More like – off-center. Maybe we just needed to talk about what we'd done.

Maybe I needed to confirm that it had been everything she'd wanted.

Or had at least been enough for her.

But, no – that wasn't the whole equation. I wasn't feeling needy anymore, not like I'd been back at Colsen. Sure, I wanted to be with her, be near her – know her like that all over again. Yet the distance I felt from her at that moment didn't all boil down to what existed between us.

It went deeper than that.

It came from elsewhere.

I kind of think it actually came from me...

* * *

I fell asleep on that car ride. It had been so many years since I'd done that. On so many long, sunny days as a little kid, sleep would greet me in the car so easily...just roll on up like a wave onto the sand. You get older, that doesn't happen anymore. Something gets drier inside. You have more on your mind. You can't just expect or trust that your parents are holding absolutely everything in your world together.

As a little kid, though, expecting and trusting that is key to your survival...

I remembered a day with Grandpa Angus. Random day, probably a Sunday, I think. I was 11 years old. He'd taken me to the beach. I couldn't remember why. But that day, although ordinary as it unfolded, had become so special in my mind's eye. It was like the perfect passage of my childhood. We hadn't even done anything magnificent. Walked on the sand. I'd run into the water. No Jordan around. No Grandma, no parents. I think we might have kicked a soccer ball back and forth. Then Grandpa, before bringing me back to the car, had bought me a hot dog and French fries and soda. It had all tasted so good after running around most of the day underneath the beautiful, radiant sunshine.

Then on the ride home that day, I'd fallen asleep.

He was so strong, Angus. Filled up my world with his might. Eleven years old, I looked at him as a god of some kind. The kind of god you could fall asleep next to because you had no doubt that he was taking care of everything during your slumber.

He'd get you home okay.

Tuck you into bed, maybe.

I'll never forget that day, for as long as I live.

* * *

The older me's Saturday ride home was a little different. My sleep in the car hadn't been bad, but when I woke from it, I felt overcome by a strange sourness. Maybe 'cause I'd mixed fluids with another person? Or maybe 'cause I was older now, in a vulnerable body, and I knew that I'd never again catch that feeling of peace that had gripped me on that day at the beach.

I was in my own bed when I woke. It was almost a miracle, for my being there meant my dad had carried me up. Not Jordan – he wasn't strong enough. My mom? Forget it. Don't make me laugh.

So my dad had been around, and carried me.

And I couldn't recall so much as blinking my eyes and catching but a sliver of his face.

Did he carry me out of guilt? Did he even think about the night before?

I loved my dad, then, but to love him meant hurting. So I scooped up my phone from the bed: fully charged now. I sighed with relief upon seeing that Rebecca had finally called to see where I was just around the time when my mom and I had left to find my dad. I couldn't bear to listen to her message, though. To hear the way she sounded in the not-so-distant past, prior to both our lives changing forever...that would have been too much for me at that moment.

I scrolled through my numbers. Past the movie club guys. My thumb hovered over each of their names, but – no.

I didn't want to tell anyone.

Had Rebecca called someone? Probably Stacy. Yeah – it was hard to imagine her not having *at least* told Stacy. Or...

I gulped at the thought...

Was she embarrassed? Maybe it was too strange. Although Stacy had known we were glued to each other, maybe this kind of news, with this kind of guy, was difficult to broadcast.

Trickier still: Was that why *I* wasn't telling people?

Did I fear on some level that they'd disbelieve me?

Nah, especially not the movie club crew. For my money, every last one of those guys was still a virgin. They'd be eager to hear a story about sex no matter who or what the source was.

Still, though...

My phone thudded onto the carpet.

Then footsteps thudded by in the hall.

Jordan...

"Jordan!"

He popped open the door half a second later. "Hey bro," he said. "Sorry. Was in a rush..."

"It's okay."

I looked at him. The look went on for like 20 seconds. Awk-ward.

He blinked. "You all right, bro?"

"Huh?"

He stepped toward me, waved a palm before my face: "Earth to Tucker."

I forced a smile. Or half of one. "Yeah. I just woke up."

He nodded again as he stepped back toward the door and put his hand on its edge. Before exiting, he turned and asked, "Why'd you call me in here?"

Now it was I who was blinking. Should I tell him? Should I tell him? Should I--

"Nothing," I said. "I'll tell you later."

He squinted a little. Less curious than just trying to be funny.

Then he walked away, saying, "Okay," as he shut the door.

Guy didn't even care to know.

* * *

ROLLING HOME

Want to hear a cliché?

Okay: Here's a cliché for you...

Everything happens for a reason.

Stick with me here, 'cause I might have one or two original words to say on this particular subject...

Everything *has to* happen for a reason. For once something happens – that's it. It can't not happen. It's in the books. Part of the fabric.

Forever.

So since every happening is so necessary to the grand quilt that makes up reality, there has to be a reason behind it – not from a romantic point-of-view, but from a practical point-of-view.

For every single happening is part of the puzzle.

See, reality is what it is. No more, no less. When something's real, it's real. It factors into the overall equation of reality. Be that as it may, one has two choices:

One can say that nothing ever happens for a reason, or that everything happens for a reason. But you can't have it both ways. You can't say that some things happen for a reason and that other things don't. No – that would be too choppy, and defy basic logic.

If you choose to say nothing ever happens for a reason – even though everything that happens has weight, on account of being a happening – then that's fine, that's entirely up to you. Your preferences are your own.

However, if you go the other way, and factor in the

major weight – the necessary quality – of every occurrence, then you're left with the striking possibility that occurrences are tied to reasons.

Either one lives in a chaotic world, or a meaningful one.

Either way, the cool part is: The world is what we make of it.

In my world, everything happens for a reason. Just one giant puzzle, where every piece not only fits, but has a definable purpose – if not more than one. Do I think this way because I exist in a wheelchair? Perhaps.

Or perhaps because I exist in a wheelchair, I realize how important and life-affirming it is to think this way...Hmm...

Anyway, that trip to San Diego was like a pit in my soul: I was dreading it. No purpose, no urgency, no joy to be expected. My father had just given the lamest alcoholic performance of his lifetime on Friday night, my brother was getting way too old for this stuff, Grandpa Angus wasn't joining on account of his chronic shame, and as for me, I was so strung out on the high of losing my virginity that I could barely string two coherent thoughts together...

But there we were, for some reason: A family, going off together on a trip.

Yet in the end, I realized that we didn't just go for "some reason."

We went for a very specific reason.

A reason, in fact, that would change my life...

ROLLING HOME

We went to San Diego so that I could meet Kip Cruiser.

* * *

"Racecar driving?!"

I couldn't help but smile.

"Racecar driving," my dad repeated.

But whereas I'd capped off my words with a question mark, he capped off his with a very resonant period.

Then he held up the tickets: bright, crisp, colorful cardboard rectangles.

"I'm not going," my mom said, shaking her head.

"What are you gonna do?" I asked her.

"Stay here in the room. Read!"

My dad leaned over and kissed her on the cheek. "You're electrifying, baby. That's why I married you."

"Gross!" said Jordan.

"Yeah," my mom shot back, "you married me 'cause I'm not electrifying enough. You need somebody to keep you stable."

She patted him on the behind. I looked at Jordan, who shook his head. "Okay," he said, moving toward the door. "I'm definitely way too old for these vacations..."

My thoughts exactly.

"Where are you going?" my dad asked Jordan.

"Car!" said Jordan. "Aren't we going to the races?"

"That's my boy!"

We all filed out, except for my mom, who was in for a much-needed dose of peace and quiet.

* * *

Yeah, my dad was trying too hard.

There was really no other way to interpret his behavior. The last thing he was mentally or emotionally prepared to do was speak to us directly about his problem, so I suppose the next best thing was for him to act all cool and spirited.

Or at least try his best to.

He did a good, solid job of it. Even though it was a bit exhausting to see him so "on" for every second of that trip, I could only imagine how much energy *he* needed to act that way – how deep inside he had to reach to conjure up all that enthusiasm and good cheer for his family's sake.

In fact, across seven whole days, he only managed to screw up once...

And it wasn't even a real screw-up, just a technical one.

"Motorcycles??"

This was Jordan speaking.

My dad plucked the tickets from his breast pocket and studied them. "Just says auto racing here," he said.

Jordan rolled his eyes, but I think he was putting on a show.

"I think it's cool," I said.

"Well thank you, son."

My dad looked at Jordan, telegraphing with his gaze that he'd called *me* son, but not him. They held their eye contact for about a second before they both smiled and laughed.

"I was just hoping to see a car flip over," said Jordan, as we started crossing the turnstiles. As a matter of course, a security guard stepped to a black steel gate and snapped it open so as to allow my passage.

"You can see a bike flip over instead," my dad said, patting Jordan on the back as I followed them in.

Unbeknownst to me at that moment, right on the other side of that gate, a new hero of mine awaited...

* * *

Kip Cruiser was the guy in the orange jacket.

All the other racers wore darker colors: most of them black, a couple of them brown or gray, and one of them red, but for Kip it was orange, and that made him stand out.

Which is not to say he needed any help from his color...

The guy was a real sight to behold. Now I'll be honest here: I couldn't really follow the races. I didn't know how the judges were keeping score. I just knew from about two minutes in that that guy in the orange jacket was the star of the show.

He just seemed to have the force of God behind him. His bike was not only faster than the others – it seemed propelled by a higher form of energy.

There was just an aura wrapped around Kip Cruiser.

You didn't have to be an incredibly perceptive person to pick up on the fact that he was the main attraction. It was just obvious, the same way it'd be if you were sitting on the floor of Congress and the President of the United States walked in.

People carried Kip Cruiser posters. People wore his grinning face on their T-shirts. People cheered just that much louder when he blurred across the finish line.

Kip was a staple of the racetrack's very atmosphere. It was a big place: an outdoor track with maybe 5,000 spectators on hand. Lots of noise. Lots of smoke. Always noisier during the races, not just due to the cheering, but because of those engines.

Aggressive. Propulsive. They cut you deep.

But despite all the sensory data in that place, Kip somehow managed to be the first thing on everybody's mind. I don't mean to make him sound like more than he was – he was only human, after all – and to be honest, had I just been an ordinary spectator, watching the races then returning home, I probably wouldn't have remembered the guy after that night. It's not like I would have gone home and suddenly became a racing fan. This was just some excursion thrown together by my dad.

But as it turned out, I wasn't just an ordinary spectator.

I was a spectator who Kip took under his wing...

* * *

"You like racing?"

It was so strange, the composure this guy had. He'd just whirled around the track two dozen or so times, and not so much as a bead of sweat was on his face, much less a bead of hesitation or choppiness in his breath.

"Yeah, it's cool," I said. "I'd never seen it before."

I'll admit that my heart-rate kicked up a little. Not because I was intimidated by his celebrity status, but because I hadn't been prepared to speak to him. And there was also the obvious factor that he'd singled me out on account of my physical condition. Was I supposed to be flattered and starstruck, or a little annoyed?

Nah – I wasn't gonna be a jerk about it. Truth was, his attention gave me some more confidence. A nice solid helping, right atop the confidence I'd already been granted by Rebecca.

We were positioned near a gate that led out to the racetrack. It was short – waist-high for an average person on foot. A couple of security guards stood near it, faces stern and shoulders up near their ears – ready to pounce and do some damage if they had to. When Kip came over after the races, everybody cheered and a bunch of people swarmed in like bees to honey. As a matter of course, they were careful to keep their distance from my chair. I'd like to think that instinct on their part came from compassion, but the truth was it probably came from fear. Fear of hurting me, fear of having to interact with me...

But Kip Cruiser exhibited no such fear.

I was the very first person he acknowledged. I had no pad and pen at the ready, unlike about 20 of the people around us, so I obviously wasn't angling for an autograph. That factor in no way deterred him, though.

It was almost as though he had come over just for me.

"What's your name?"

"Tucker."

"Tucker. I'm Kip."

We shook hands. Unlike every single person whose hand I'd shaken after my accident, he didn't recoil or pause upon realizing that my hand was in less than tip-top condition. Even Grandpa Angus, God bless him, had let me down with a pause. Though I suppose it was understandable since he'd pulled the trigger...

"Ever hear of murderball?"

I couldn't believe how much talking he was doing with me when so many dozens – maybe hundreds – of other people wanted his attention right at that moment. The perks you get when you get hurt, I guess...

The best part was, as eager as the fans were to speak with him, the fact that he was speaking with me made them all keep a good bit of distance. Had I just been some regular kid, there would have no doubt been elbows, pads, and pens all up in Kip's face. On account of who I was, however – and what I looked like – they collectively decided to grant me this little moment.

"I've heard of it, yeah."

"Ever played it?"

"No."

Then it happened. A girl in a tight top stepped up to Kip, pad in aim. "I'm like your biggest fan," she laughed, clearly drunk out of her mind.

He took the pad from her but kept his eyes on me:

"Wait over there," he said, clicking his chin toward a trashcan outside the Men's Room. "I want to talk to you...Just be a minute..."

I paused. I let my gaze blend into his. According to my intuition, this guy wasn't just being casual. He actually wanted to talk.

"Okay," I said, then I rolled off, leaving Kip to his people.

* * *

"Hey, that was pretty cool," my dad smiled, his buoyant mood still wholly intact.

"What do you think he wants to talk about?" asked Jordan.

"No idea," I said, my eyes drilling into the crowd around Kip. I couldn't see the man himself anymore, but the statement of orange he wore around himself wasn't easy to lose track of.

As it turned out, predictably, Kip's "minute" became more like 20 minutes. I never got tired of waiting, though. Truth be told, I was eager to hear what he had to say. As we waited, Dad and Jordan talked about the races, explaining to each other and to themselves how the sport worked and why it was entertaining. As for me, I didn't chime in too much; I was too busy getting ready for my next encounter with the star.

When he came over, finally, he started off with small talk: Where were we from? What did my dad do? What brought us to the races? Then, after a couple of minutes of that stuff, when he finally got going with me again, he said something that I'll never forget:

"We're the same," he said.

I smiled. "How are we the same?"

"Life on wheels, right?"

We laughed. "Yeah," I agreed, "only mine go slower."

"Not if you play murderball," he said.

"That's some name," my dad interjected.

"Oh, it's fun," Kip told him, waving his hand. "I've coached guys playing it a bunch of times. Couple of girls – or women – too."

My dad looked down at me, eyebrows raised. "Hey – now that does sound cool. Mr. Cruiser here could be your coach."

"Please – Kip. My friends call me Kip."

"Well I'd be honored if you coached Tucker, Kip."

Kip gave my dad a grin, but turned the floor back to me: "You like the sound of it?"

I wasn't about to commit right there on the spot. Naturally, a little bit of research was necessary, the better to make sure I didn't end up in a situation where I ended up dead. Just the same, I said, "Sounds cool. You gotta tell me more..."

* * *

And that was the start of my friendship with Kip Cruiser.

The rest of San Diego was a slow-paced blur. Slow because the stops were nothing special: restaurants, stores, couple houses belonging to my mom's aunts and cousins. Blurry because my mind wasn't really along for the trip. Dangling there before my mind's eye, at practically every waking moment, were two key figures:

Rebecca and Kip.

Rebecca kept texting and calling throughout my time away. Sometimes I answered or replied right away; other times I let a few hours slip by. Though I was excited about seeing her again, the trip helped me realize an age-old truth...

If I may use a racing metaphor: Being in the chase was more exciting than crossing the finish line.

There: I said it. Hate to be the zillionth guy who's had that thought, particularly in light of how honored I was that she'd shared herself with me. But now that the screen of mania about consummating our relationship was gone – now that that part of my brain was no longer all charged up with urgency – I was able to see through to another reality beyond it:

The possibility, once so remote, that I could actually have *options* when it came to females...

Granted, I didn't have any real-life, physical options at that moment, so getting cocky was definitely out of the question. But having proven that I could make love to a girl, and that I could therefore be a normal person, opened up new avenues of normalcy in my mind. And once these avenues were open, I allowed myself to look at Rebecca from a more rational and grounded perspective.

In other words: Was she right for me? Did we truly click? Was she comfortable with me because I was limited? Did my compromised state inspire some confidence or even bravery on her part? If so, was that acceptable? Did such things happen, on some level, in all relationships?

I wasn't about to nail down a bunch of answers to these questions right away. A lot of exploring still lay ahead. For now, the main thing was that I felt bad. Downright shitty, in fact.

What kind of a jerk was I being?

* * *

"You're not a jerk!" Jordan said, then he vanished under the water.

It was the last night of our San Diego trip. It occurred to me, then, in the suffocating desert air, that this would probably be the last-ever trip for our family – that is, as a unit of four. Maybe I'd go more places with my parents, but Jordan's status as the kid who was too old was definitely something all of us were tuned into. Then soon I myself would be too old. Then there'd be a whole new era: Jordan and me in our own places, probably, and my parents taking the kind of trips that empty-nesters go on: Palm Springs, Miami, maybe some cruises.

That is, if they were still together.

I got a hard chill. Despite my dad's able performance throughout the week, it was foolish to think he'd just be able to drop his addiction like there was nothing to it. And if he didn't, how much more could my mom take? Moreover, how much could his two sons take? What would have to happen before we all just turned on him, and demanded he go and seek out another way of life?

Was that feasible? Was I dreaming?

Did I *want* that to happen?

Anyway, the fact that it was probably our last family vacation wrecked me with a degree of sentimentality that I hadn't been prepared for. I'd been so tied up thinking about Rebecca and then Kip that contemplating my family as a unit hadn't really been my most pressing order of business. Yet there could be no mistaking it:

Everything was changing now.

Not only had my physical being been altered, the world around me was turning inside out. And I'd have to hang on pretty tight to survive this trip.

"It's okay if you think I am," I said.

Jordan popped up out of the pool, spraying some water on my legs in the process.

"What?" he asked, wiping his nose with his hand.

I repeated myself: "It's – okay – if – you – think – I – am."

"Bro..." He set his arms on the edge of the pool. "...do you really think I'd hesitate to call you a jerk?"

The two of us laughed.

"So how do you characterize a guy that has sex with a girl and then feels a clear reduction in interest?"

"Gosh, you're all talking like a scientist and sh--"

"I'm serious!" Though I was smiling.

"What do I call a guy like that? Oh, I don't know: HUMAN, maybe?"

I looked away, shaking my head.

He went on: "That's just how things go, little bro.

It's like peeling away the layers of an onion..."

I looked back at him. "What is?"

"What isn't?" he shrugged. "Life, relationships. Everything. You're always learning. The learning never stops. You cross a barrier, you find new things. Inside yourself, outside yourself. The only way you avoid that is by standing still. And even if you do that, you learn the cost of standing still. There's no way to keep the learning out."

"So what's the lesson here, then? That I don't love her? That I'm not ready for this?"

"Dude: It's not like the lessons get thrown at your feet in nice little bundles. You have to keep living this thing, keep learning this stuff. And do you want some hard truth?"

"Sure. I can take it." I smiled with my eyes. He knew what I meant.

"Stop thinking about her so much!"

After he said this, he cupped some water up in his hand and threw it at me. Only Jordan could get away with that. Anybody else, it would have been a case of assault or something. All I could do in my defense was spring my arms up and shut my eyes.

"You want my opinion? Next move: murderball. Get the blood flowing in other parts of your body..."

He was right, of course.

Courtesy of Kip Cruiser, I had a chance to change my aperture. I didn't know if that meant murderball per se, but I was looking forward to my planned follow-up with Kip.

Destination: Los Angeles.

Two weeks later.

Kip had invited me up to his house in the hills.

CHAPTER 7

Rolling

I t should come as no surprise that Kip Cruiser was the source of my very first fight with Rebecca...

"I don't, like, understand," she said. And if I'm not mistaken, those were actual tears in her eyes...

"Can you, like, keep your voice down?" I said.

We were in her bedroom – not on the bed. By then, I'd been home for 12 days. We'd slept together probably six more times. I still felt close to her, and I still liked her. I don't know about "loved" or anything like that, but being with her was definitely about more than just my confidence level. It felt nice to be with her, nice to make *her* feel nice. And the rhythm between us was smooth and true.

Yet now we were hitting the rocks on account of

Kip.

Her position: I should have invited her along.

My position: This was something I had to go do on my own.

"Look, you gotta understand: I'm on a journey here with this thing. Do you get me?"

She nodded. The tears slid down her cheeks.

I went on, "I have to live with myself this way. And that means discovering myself. And there are gonna be things I want to discover on my own..."

I hoped that by framing my words in the future tense, I'd get the message across that I planned on being with her for a while. Hopefully that would grant her a sense of peace, and help her to not feel excluded.

"But all we do," she said, "is hang out here lately..."

"I know. You're right."

"And you were just gone for a week, and now it's gonna be a weekend--"

"Baby," I said. I touched her hair. "I'll be back before you know it."

* * *

Amazing, how true Jordan's words had been.

Life was a teacher, no doubt about it. And the lesson plan was forever open-ended...

I'll admit it: I had been needy as could be before Rebecca and I finally got together. But if I'm willing to admit that, then I also have to cut myself some slack. I mean: I had only just been through the most brutal transition of my lifetime. At the time, she'd been a lifeline for me.

And now, with the script flipped, and her being the needy one...what did I represent to her? Truly?

I supposed I'd have to ask her someday.

For now, however, it was all about the weekend at Kip's place.

My mom had checked him out on the Internet. The guy was 1,000 percent legit. If he had sinister intentions, they would come as a major surprise. He had a live-in girlfriend, and his 19-year-old nephew stayed with them, too, when he wasn't away at college (which he would be that weekend). Kip's ranch, just north of Hollywood, was where he trained kids and adults alike to compete in murderball. That wasn't the objective of my visit, though – at least not officially. No, the plan was for him to introduce me to murderball, but to also serve as something of a life coach, providing a much-needed dose of inspiration.

For when Kip wasn't inspiring people out on the track, he was inspiring them from behind a podium, giving speeches at high schools and colleges and corporations about leading an inspired life.

I hardly knew the guy, but already I loved him.

Plus, he was qualified to care for a disabled person. He had ample experience, knew all the precautions and procedures.

When my mom dropped me off, she said to call if

I needed anything.

Translation: "Call if you find yourself tied to a chair or something."

I smiled at her as she gave me a kiss. Considering how far south things had gone the last time she'd let me go away with an adult for the weekend, we could probably depend on my luck being slightly better this time.

* * *

"Why murderball?" I asked.

We were out in his backyard, baking in the midday L.A. sun. In keeping with our topic of conversation, Kip held what looked to be a volleyball in his hands. Seeing him out of his racing gear, I saw he kept his arms in good shape. It occurred to me that bike racing, however mechanical by nature, still required a high degree of physical fitness.

I was inspired by it. The idea of having big, lethal arms was one that very much appealed to me. Right there on the spot, I turned it into a personal goal.

"It's more polite name is wheelchair rugby," he said.

"Oh, so it's like football," I replied.

He shook his head. "Only in the sense that the object is to get the ball over the line. But you're on a hardwood floor, *naturally*..."

I gave him a nod.

"...and indoors."

"Okay," I said, then grinned. "So *why murderball?*"

He nodded before answering: "Because it's tough."

"So I've heard."

"But it's not, perhaps, as tough as you've heard. You're safe out there: your chair is fortified. Ever seen 'Mad Max'?"

"Sure. The new one," I said, meaning "Mad Max: Fury Road", but lying: I hadn't seen any of those movies. I made a mental note to put 'em on our movie club queue.

"Okay," he went on, "so you know what I mean: Your chair's all armored up. You're protected. Which is not to say I don't see guys fracture their fingers and stuff like that. It *can* get rough. But I think this whole 'murder' thing is something they just use to sell tickets."

"Fair enough," I said. "How do you play?"

* * *

Picture basketball, hockey, handball, and rugby all mashed up into an intense 30-minute game, with spinal cord injury patients playing in wheelchairs on a hardwood court, and you're in the vicinity of what murderball consists of. Twelve players a team, but only four per team on the court at the same time. Your team's objective is to get the ball over the other team's goal line. In the course of doing so, you can bash your wheelchair into those of the other players – who may be male or may even be female – but within limits. You can't just ram into someone from behind, for example. Nor can you get all "handsy" out there, grabbing another player directly.

However, the wheelchair contact is a big part of the game's fascination, for the players and the fans alike. At first glance, it may seem like the game is exploitation – kind of like a Roman coliseum event where everyone gathers just to see horror and carnage – but it's actually not that at all. It takes strategy and dexterity to play in a wheelchair. As for the sport's more violent elements, they're a source of pride for the players, 'cause they give us an opening to show the audience that we're not weak.

Yeah, I liked every bit of what Kip told me about murderball.

On that initial afternoon at his house, we worked a few drills wherein he showed me how to maneuver in my chair while holding the ball. It was tricky on account of my compromised hands; I had to keep at least one hand operating the chair and do my best to tuck the ball under my armpit while in motion. The impact of another player – or worse, an incident of sheer clumsiness on my part – could mean the ball ended up on the floor.

Speaking of that floor, it was a legitimate hardwood court, complete with its own distinct patterns, sections, and goal lines. The layout resembled those we're used to seeing on basketball and hockey courts, but it still had its own exotic stamp and personality. Moreover, Kip had his very own court right there on his property. When he opened the door to his private murderball center and showed me in, I knew full well this guy was legit. Not only did the presence of the court mean he was loaded with cash, it also meant he was serious about the game – possibly as serious as he was about motorcycle racing.

"How did you get into this?" I asked him after our initial training session, sipping soda by a table positioned at the side of the court.

"I told ya when I met ya," said Kip, hissing out a breath after taking his own sip. "We have a natural bond."

"Yeah, okay: We're both on wheels. But how does somebody's mind get from motorcycles to wheelchairs?"

Kip stood up, patting my knee as he rose. "I live for speed, dude. It's God's greatest gift to me. When I think about guys like you, who have that either taken way or trampled on, it makes me angry. So this..." He did a little twirl, pointing out the court that filled the center. "...is how I make things better."

"Do you have a preference?"

He looked at me, brows lowering.

I clarified: "Murderball or racing?"

Kip shrugged. "Good question. The truth?"

I nodded.

"I think pretty soon: Murderball."

* * *

I met the reason behind his answer about 15 minutes later.

Her name was Monica, and if I thought Kip had it all before, then I thought he had it all and then some when I met her.

She was not only beautiful, she was smart.

And not only smart, but genuinely kind. And funny. And...

I had to do all that I could to not fall in love.

Monica was Kip's girlfriend, but they seemed so domestically settled and cozy that she may as well have been his wife. She was in their giant, classy kitchen preparing lunch when we came back inside. We ate tuna fish sandwiches while Kip told a couple of stories about his races around the world. It sounded like the guy's schedule was completely crazy: He was due in Japan the day after I left (which was the following day), then Cairo a week after that, then back to the states for a few days, then down to Brazil...

And the most freakish part was what my mom had learned online:

He never lost.

Or if he did, then that must have occurred in a previous lifetime. Despite zigzagging all around the globe

– despite probably being jetlagged and exhausted from sitting on all those planes and breathing in all that fake, stale air – when Kip got on his bike, he was about a half-inch shy of a god. He just *made it happen*: anytime, anywhere.

And there at his side, along with his manager and crew, was Monica.

But as Kip would tell me after lunch, as we made the rounds about his immense property, Monica was getting just a little bit tired of the ride.

"Oh man," I said, feeling his pain.

"I know," he said.

We were making our way down a path lined with trees. The way the light sprinkled in through the cracks in the foliage put me in a mystical frame of mind. This place seemed...holy, or something like that. Even Kip and Monica had such strong lights around them.

Just happy people, living how they wanted.

I was buckling with gratitude over having met them.

"So I figure," said Kip, as we made our way, "I put one more year into this. Biking's a young man's sport anyway. You cross 30, they look at you like you're a senior citizen."

"So you'll coach murderball? Seriously?"

He shrugged. "Why not?"

"It just seems...wow. Whole new life."

"Ah, life is always new, my friend. It never gets situated. It's always in motion..."

We progressed toward the end of the path, where a fountain awaited. I thought of what Jordan had said, about the life experience just being one ongoing, open-ended learning process. Kip's words squared somewhat with those of Jordan. I sensed the universe was giving me a message through those two guys. Something to do with being open to the ride, letting it do what it may, letting its wisdom and fury just flow right in.

I was open to it. Excited by it, too. But also scared, deep down inside. Day in and day out, this notion that I wasn't normal was getting firmer and tighter inside my being. Sure, I could talk normal. And yes, God had gifted me a wonderful girlfriend, but how could I get back to a place where I just felt comfortable inside my life? Where I never even considered the topic of normalcy because I took it for granted that I was normal?

Just like I had for all those years before the accident.

"Do you want to change, though? In your heart?" I asked him.

We were positioned near the edge of the fountain now. A statue of Cupid, bow and arrow in aim, stood tall and fat above the water, its mouth acting as a faucet that never got shut off. I figured this contribution to the property had been Monica's...or perhaps something Kip had installed after they fell in love.

He had to think about my question. His eyelids drew downward. This close to him – a couple feet away – I saw pretty much for the first time how much natural charisma he had. He could have been on TV or in movies if he wanted to. Well, I guess he *was* on TV all the time, but the point was that it seemed like God had made this guy for fame. Just being near him, being in his aura, made me feel this strange, yet undeniable power.

"It's earlier than I would like," he told me. "My choice? I'd give it three or five more years. Not one. It's happening..." He sucked in his breath, then whistled it back out. "...pretty fast, bud. I guess that's God telling me that even *I* get scared of speed sometimes."

He winked at me. I smiled.

At that instant, courtesy of that brief exchange, I felt in my gut that Kip was a true friend, and not just some charity dispenser trying to wrestle down his own guilt. Not only was his way of addressing me entirely unforced and fluent, but he'd just told me something that I didn't think Monica would have wanted to hear.

So just like that, we were close.

Or real friends, at least.

In the minutes that followed, I told him all about Rebecca. He and Jordan were now the only ones who knew what had happened, but Kip got the full story, from beginning to...well, not end – but up 'til now.

He was as shocked as you'd expect someone to be. Delighted, actually. The more I went into the more intimate details, the more he appreciated what he was hearing. Not from a weird or creepy standpoint, but from a position of being impressed by how I'd transcended my limitations.

"But now the question is," I said, "do I stick with her because it works, or explore other options?"

He thought about it. I sensed the wheels in his mind at work, as he wasn't only weighing the age-old, classic elements of my question, but the factor of me being in a wheelchair, and thus having a trickier road ahead of me in terms of actually orchestrating options. Before he answered, having intuited what he was thinking, I said, "I mean, don't get me wrong: I know I might not have other options, ever..."

Then he looked at me. He seemed...not annoyed, but definitely not exactly happy. "Why do you say that?" he asked.

"'Cause...I don't know. Look at me."

"Look at you? Look at what? Your handsome face?"

"Don't flatter a guy."

"What would I gain by flattering you, Tucker? The second a person – any person – starts perceiving limited options in their life, guess what happens?"

I waited.

He finished: "Your options start to dwindle away."

"Okay, but that's an attitude thing," I said, thinking back to all my days with Tony. "I'm talking plain truth. My body..."

"Your body's broken, sure. Not dead, though."

"Limited."

"Um, did you not hear the story you just told me?"

"Ha! I did. And I kind of suspect it's the story of a dude who fell into some luck..."

"Kind of a funny spin to put on your grandfather having shot you."

"I'm talking about Rebecca."

"I get it. But you're not following me, Tucker." Kip stood up from the edge of the fountain and gestured with his hands as he continued, "Limitations are purely perceptual. Always. One hundred percent of the time."

"My neck got broken!" I wasn't yelling, just exclaiming. Truth be told, I was enjoying Kip's philosophical nature.

"Duh, I can see that. But that's not a limitation."

"Why not?"

"'Cause it's all in how you spin it."

"Explain."

"Really?"

I nodded.

"Okay." He went on, "I know you're smart enough to know this already, but just for the sake of humoring you: Your objective, in this case, is to have more options in terms of female companions. Totally natural, eternal male impulse. Yet you're worried that...what's her name, again?"

"Rebecca."

"You're worried that Rebecca's like some once-in-a-lifetime, unicorn-level occurrence, that'll never repeat itself because SOMEHOW – despite having been SHOT – you walk around thinking you're this incredibly lucky person..."

"In terms of her."

"I got it, yes: In terms of her. But Tucker: Your injury did not limit you here, nor will it. Your injury will help you."

"How?"

"Do you know what women love, above all else?"

I shook my head.

"Two things: feeling safe, and being with men who are vulnerable. With you, the safety's in the bag. You can't hurt them. It's off the table. And the vulnerability's in plain sight: You were hurt. Anyone with eyes can see it. That's the hand God dealt you, and naturally, it's a kind of lousy one on various levels. But on this level, dude...

"You can only score."

* * *

I couldn't sleep that night.

No wonder the guy was famous: He wasn't just a great bike rider, he was some kind of light-spewing visionary.

I mean: Don't get me wrong. It's not like I'm some clueless dolt. I'd been fully aware for weeks now that my physical state was arguably enticing to Rebecca for the very reasons he'd made clear.

But it's one thing to suspect something, or kind of/maybe/somewhat suspect something, and another thing entirely to have somebody else lay it out for you, loud and clear.

This was quite possibly the happiest I'd been since that bullet had left that gun.

It wasn't like I was about to go to town being some manipulator of female emotions, wheeling around the neighborhood dispensing sob stories about how harmless and vulnerable I was, but at least, as Kip had said, I wasn't dead.

I was still in the game.

I didn't have to be tied down with one person on account of some perceptual limitations. In fact, being tied down was something that grown-ups experienced. You end up in a marriage, then get tied down by the source of income, or the house you own together, or the kids you have, then maybe someday an illness – or maybe all of the above. All of that was understandable. Heck, it was even going on in my own family. My mother was in too deep with my dad to consider leaving him at this juncture. She had to stay on the ride, address the challenge.

Likewise with Kip and Monica, even. Sure, they were a pair of young, rich, exciting people with the world at their feet, but Monica had made it clear to Kip that in exchange for the love and companionship she offered, she wanted him to adapt to a more domesticated lifestyle.

Kip Cruiser! The best motorcycle racer known to man! And yet at the end of the day he was only human, which led to obligations and responsibilities.

Irony of ironies, despite my condition, I wasn't yet tied down like my mom or Kip. The awareness thereof almost made my head explode. I didn't know where I would meet new girls, much less how, but I knew I could.

Maybe murderball would play a role. Maybe it'd be like being a musician, where your presence on the stage – or in the case of the game, on the court – made you an appealing prospect. I pictured myself kicking ass on the murderball court, shattering my opponents' chairs before driving that ball across the goal line.

The whole audience roared.

The sound blew out my eardrums.

And waiting for me at court-side was a beautiful girl. I couldn't see her face, nor make out the color of her hair, but I knew she was there, waiting just for me.

Perfect. Beautiful. My girl.

And whoever she was, I knew she wasn't Rebecca.

* * *

After that weekend up at Kip's, things started getting pretty crazy pretty fast...

It was almost as though some energetic particles from Kip's field of being had landed in my own reality, and started to twist and turn it in a wilder direction.

For one thing, Rebecca didn't like the murderball idea at all.

To put it more bluntly, she hated the whole thing.

"Is this about Kip?" I asked her.

We were at the food court in the mall, as part of our new agreement to branch out more and stop letting our skin grow pale beneath the dim light of her bedroom. Which is not to say I minded being there *some* of the time...

"Yeah," she said, "it's about Kip. Like, what are you, his mascot?"

"Mascot?" My eyebrows shot up. The word ticked me off, but I wasn't about to go getting hostile. "Mascots are like animals that cheer you on from the sidelines. How am I his mascot?"

"That's not the word I mean."

"Then what *do* you mean?"

Her eyes were moistening. Not due to sadness, just from the general tension. She didn't like fighting. Nor did I. But this was most certainly a fight I was intent upon winning. No way I was going to let her take murderball from me, much less my new friend.

"I mean," she said, "he's just some rich, famous guy who's trying to act all compassionate by taking you under his wing--"

"That's ridiculous. I'm not stupid. I thought that, too. But he's way into murderball. He's got a court on his property. And he's retiring from racing soon, which means he's gonna start coaching guys like me. Rebecca:

This could be a big deal for me."

She gave me her eyes, then. All their light...all their moisture. I felt so bad for making her feel bad, but in truth I didn't think she had a leg to stand on (pun intended).

"I don't mean to be unsupportive. I just..."

"Just what?"

Her voice cracked when she spoke her next words:

"I just started getting to know you, and I don't want to lose you."

* * *

Great, terrific.

Karma really is some wild beast, ain't it?

Back at Colsen, I'd tied myself up in knots trying to make my way into this very relationship, and now that I was in it, I was feeling more stuck by the moment. Granted, it wasn't all negative – not by any means. We still had fun together. She still filled up my being with hope and confidence, to the point where sometimes I was like an empty pitcher before I went to see her, and a full one on the way back home.

But for a guy who wanted nothing more than to be normal, Rebecca was starting to seem a lot *too* normal for my taste. Clingy, needy, interjecting into matters that had nothing to do with her.

I mean, there at the mall, I tried to explain to her how much the sport meant to me already, even though by then I'd only had two practices. Its mere existence in my life was already a source of structure. And hope, as well – which I frankly needed as much of as humanly possible. To my mind, the fact that a sport existed in which wheelchair-bound people could thrive was nothing shy of a miracle. Imagine that: Me coming off like a badass on the court, showing the world what I was made of:

Strength. Speed. Agility. Timing. Wit.

Like I said: No way Rebecca would take that from me.

The conversation ended on a low note. I didn't back down, but neither did she. I inwardly gave her props for not citing a concern about my safety as her leading motive. However, part of me kind of wished she *had* played that card, for the alternative card – the one where she was worried about me changing – was atrocious.

Just like Jordan had said, life was all about learning. And as we learn, we change – there's just no other way. For Rebecca to throw that kind of shackle around my ankle, in light of all I'd gone through, left me feeling bitterly cold.

Meanwhile, back among my other peers, things weren't all too warm, either...

* * *

The movie club kind of fell apart after the New Year.

The problem was, the library stuffed us in a different room. The one we'd been used to meeting in was nice and roomy, but apparently it had now been scheduled up by a church group of some kind. So my bros and I got put in an alternative room that was about the size of two closets put side-by-side. This was particularly troubling for me, as I couldn't get through the door without practically paying with my life: bending my chair almost sideways to squeeze all its parts through.

After two weeks of that nonsense, we started doing it at Anthony's house, but I guess the human species doesn't really dig change too much, 'cause nobody showed up but me, Anthony, and Tim.

The evening's selection was the third "Mad Max", the one with Tina Turner. The series was cool enough on its own, but extra awesome when I pictured all different funky fortifications on my wheelchair during a game of murderball. I'd emailed Kip while he was traveling about how my movie club was watching those films, and he'd been so excited to hear it that I think he may have broke the exclamation point key on his computer.

As a side note, in the course of replying, he'd told me there was a murderball game coming up on February 1.

And he'd invited me to compete.

I replied within 30 seconds to say I was in. No sooner had I pressed Send then I was awash in anxiety, but it was the good kind of anxiety.

The kind that happens when you're testing your-self. Pushing to and then beyond your limits.

In fact, I was so excited about playing that I could-n't sleep. Murderball became such a fixation for me that once the credits started rolling on the third "Mad Max", I had to break some bad news to my pals:

"I think we should take a break for a while."

They looked at each other, then at me.

Devastated.

I'm not saying they started crying and holding each other, but I am saying that the air in Anthony's living room got pretty dense in about a microsecond.

"You're ditching us?"

"Not ditching. We should still hang out. But – I don't know. I kind of joined this club to get out of the house, and I've got other things getting me out lately."

"Like your girlfriend?" This was Anthony talking. He sprinkled the g-word with no small amount of spite.

"Yeah, Rebecca...and..."

I looked from Anthony to Tim and then back again. For the first time, I told them all about Kip Cruiser. Granted, I'd already mentioned how cool it had been to see him race and to hang with him up at his ranch, but I hadn't gone into our plans, much less what they meant to me.

To their credit, my buddies were positive about it. After all, how much can you stomp on a handicapped guy's aspirations? At the same time, there could be no mistaking the fact that me pulling the plug on our movie nights was a heart-breaker for them. I tried to crack it up to the workings of the cosmos: First we'd lost our room at the library, then we'd lost most of our actual club members, etc...

But for them it was just another nail in the coffin.

* * *

When I got home that night, I went from feeling lousy to feeling downright abysmal.

My mom was pacing the kitchen floor, her feet stuffed in slippers and an actual *cigarette* dangling from her lips. Jordan had been the one to drive me home, but I alone had noticed my mom's rare state, as Jordan had taken off up the steps in an antsy blur.

I wheeled over, saw she had her cell phone fused against her ear.

She looked at me. Her eyes shined redness.

My own eyes widened. I held her gaze and mouthed the word "What?"

She just shook her head and kept on pacing...

About 20 seconds later, she started talking, but none of it made any sense to me. Nonetheless, with her every word I grew more alarmed:

"Okay...Okay, thank you...Yes, I'll be there...Do I need money?...Yes...I understand..."

Judging from her tone, her pace, her gaze, and the

fact that she never, ever smoked cigarettes, despite keeping packs around the same way some people keep fire extinguishers around, I could only arrive at the presumption that this was serious.

When she hung up, and started to weep, she proved me right.

The long and short of it was, more or less, what I'd deduced:

My dad was about to spend the night in jail.

* * *

All we knew at that moment was that he'd been at a bar and ended up introducing his knuckles to the face of a fellow patron. At which point the fellow patron's teeth got their own introduction to the floor. At which point my dad's body got its second-ever introduction to the back of a police car.

The first time had happened before I was born. I always liked the story, 'cause it made my dad sound tough. He and my mom had been in line to get into a concert. My mom was pregnant with Jordan at the time. Some rude guys shoved past them to make their way into the stadium, bumping into my mom's stomach in the process. My mom's skin turned red; she eyed my dad.

My dad turned to the leader of their pack and punched his lights out.

Soon the cops came and carted a handful of them

away, after which my dad ended up having to sweep the sidewalk for eight Saturdays in a row.

Back then, he'd been young and rebellious and full of life, and his behavior had just been an outgrowth of his love for my mother.

Right now, though, we were living through a different age.

Nowadays, Dad's behavior tended to be designed around avoiding his family. Accordingly, one would be hard-pressed to conclude that he'd had some noble reason for punching this new guy.

No, it'd be much easier to conclude that he was simply acting like a bum.

* * *

But as bad as this was – as much fury as my dad's recent behavior ignited in me, as much pain as my mom's reactions caused me, as much uncertainty hung over our heads as a result of this guy's problems, as gut-wrenching as it was to picture my own father locked up in a tiny cell – *nothing* compared to the agony of what my mom would have to do next.

She was going to have to go to Grandpa and ask for bail money.

The amount, she said, was $7,500. By any measure, that sounded high, but in the current circumstances it also sounded like whatever Dad had done hadn't been something that could just get swept under the rug.

No – the feeling I got, on that grim, oppressive night, was that we had just encountered a problem that was here to stay.

Moreover, it scared me that we didn't have the money. As for who we had to turn to, that was only about 3,000 times more petrifying.

In a perfect world, Grandpa Angus would be more than happy to help, having acknowledged fully that he'd hurt me and therefore owed as much to us in return as humanly possible.

This, however – as I think we all realize by now – was not a perfect world.

This was a world in which Angus could turn on my father.

* * *

Grandpa Angus looked so old in the nighttime.

It was kind of an amazing sight to behold. It fed to me some information about the nature of the human body. So much of the time in recent years, I'd seen the man only during daylight hours. Would have seen him by night out there in the wilderness, but that plan of course got interrupted.

And now, as he stood there in the doorway, wearing his burgundy bathrobe and creasing his bushy eyebrows (Did he comb them during the day?) with concern, he looked a good 10 years older than he had the last time I'd seen him. I supposed that as one aged, one's physical form underwent some mild, nearly imperceptible level of deterioration throughout the day.

But I perceived it.

Moreover, I perceived that his expression revealed more than concern.

He was afraid.

* * *

His fear had vanished after the three of us settled in his kitchen. Good ole' Angus: He'd widened his own doorways on account of me. Had even lowered the legs on his kitchen table – an unnecessary move in terms of both physicality and generosity – just to accommodate my occasional presence. The moves not only told me how much he loved me, but made me feel right at home under his roof.

Grandma was still sleeping. She'd woken briefly to ask what was up, then drifted away pretty rapidly after Mom told her. It wasn't 'cause she didn't care; it was 'cause her hip had been bothering her lately, and she dropped some pretty serious chemicals down her hatch prior to bedtime: painkillers, sleeping pills, other stuff I couldn't comprehend.

As for Grandpa, well, he wasn't sleeping very long these days...

So it was just me, my grandpa, and my mom at that kitchen table. Angus poured me a glass of milk prior to sitting. It had been my favorite drink like 12 years prior, but I suppose in the context of his lifetime that had only been a little while ago. I drank the milk with gratitude. Something about grandparents' house has such tonal perfection. The coldness of the milk goes deeper. The richness of the vibes runs stronger.

I could tell, prior to Grandpa Angus speaking, that he was choosing his words with care. He didn't want to insult his daughter's husband, much less his grandson's father. Just the same, if the red tint of his face meant anything, he was probably a good few notches beyond furious. God knew the last thing our family needed was more drama.

Mom had explained what was happening, briefly, in the foyer. She hadn't repeated herself at all. Just plain, simple words: "He had a fight. He's in jail. We need $7,000."

Angus was no dummy; he didn't need things spelled out.

Didn't even wish to ask after why the fight had occurred.

On the one hand, such was 'cause the core origin was obvious: alcohol. On the other hand, such was 'cause Grandpa Angus – to put it simply – was a badass.

He had neither the time nor the interest for gossip.

"I'll give you the money," Grandpa Angus said.

My mom released something resembling a sigh.

"And I'm happy to. You said $7,000."

"Well, $7,500," she said.

"Okay, then: 75."

"No, but I have $500."

He waved his hand. "Let's keep it simple and clean. You just renovated your house..." He was referring to the wheelchair-access "renovations", of course. "...hang onto your cash."

"I'll pay it back," my mom said.

I'd never seen her like this before. Our family unit was entering oddball territory. I wish I could say I liked the way it felt. My dad was out there acting like a child, and as a result, my mom had been reduced to childlike requests from her own dad, and then in the middle of it all was me: The youngest one in the group, yet getting force-fed all this tricky wisdom from the fates.

Normalcy – my number-one objective, my goal to end all goals – seemed incredibly far away right then.

Meanwhile, Grandpa was waving his hand again. He said, "That's not my concern. But if I may, I'd like to voice other concerns..."

There he went getting all internal again. His eyes: far away. Those brows: in desperate need of a clip n' comb. Judging from my mom's breath, I doubted she had the patience to listen to whatever lay in store, but when a guy says he's about to put $7,500 in your hands, the courtesy of hearing him out comes with the package...

"There's two ways this thing can go right now," he said. "You're at a crossroads. It's either all downhill, or it stabilizes. So the courts, well – $7,500 indicates a fel-ony. Which indicates the possibility of jail-time."

"He has no criminal record," my mom said.

"What about when you were pregnant with Jor-dan?"

"Misdemeanor. That got wiped years ago."

"Okay. So God willing, he gets probation again. But to be honest with you both, whatever the penalty is – and I pray it isn't prison – it has to be a sincere pen-alty. Not just sweeping the roads. He needs a class. He has an illness."

My being felt like it had turned to stone. Never be-fore had I seen Dad's issue through that lens. Probably 'cause my own condition was so serious, and so phys-ically irreversible, that framing his taste for alcohol as something that couldn't be controlled seemed ridicu-lous.

But what if it couldn't be?

What if this got worse?

What if my dad was going to go away?

* * *

Grandpa Angus said some more words at that table. But none of them landed on me as hard as "illness." My faith in my caretakers was beginning to slip. No longer did I have the child's privilege of taking their power and stability for granted.

Mom begging for money.

Dad waiting for freedom.

Angus dropping that gun.

And ironically, despite Grandpa Angus having messed up worse than anyone, he was the strongest character of the bunch. Strange how life reveals such things.

Yet regardless of the man's natural strength, the truth was – as my first look at him in that doorway had confirmed – he was getting old. I could hardly depend on him to last forever.

So that was it, now.

I, too, was getting old.

And it seemed like each new day was pinning uncomfortable forms of awareness to my brain.

Maybe such was why God had put Kip inside my life. Maybe Kip was the key; my adult guide. Someone who could light my way.

I mean: Gosh, I was still just a kid. I might have had an active brain, but I still wasn't old enough to go at this life thing on my own.

Quite the contrary, I needed more help now than I ever had.

The date flashed in my head for the first time since I'd heard the news about my dad: February 1.

Just shy of a month away. Heck, call it what it was: Closer to three weeks now than four. I would have to train. Or would I even have time? Would our family's collective brain now be focused on my dad's defense?

'Cause bail was one thing...but lawyers were another.

Could I back out? Would doing so be lame – me using my family's discord as an excuse to stay inside my comfort zone?

And if I stayed there, would I alienate my new friend?

Or, I mean: Mentor?

Angus rose. He moved to the kitchen counter and got his key rings. As I heard the jingle-jangle, I processed that he was about to head to the safe and get the cash. I had no clue if this was a little or a lot for him, though I detected he was more concerned about our family's future than the matter of the money.

"Tucker stays here," he said, as he moved toward the room's doorway.

My mom turned her body to face his. Her shoulders were higher than usual. "You don't have all his stuff."

"What stuff?" Grandpa chortled for the first time since we'd walked in. "We got food and shelter. What does he need, an oxygen machine?"

I smiled.

"I don't want to impose," my mom said.

"You know what's worse for him than this place?" He didn't even have to say it, but he did: "A jail. Let's keep the poor kid's attitude elevated."

Yeah, I thought ruefully, good luck with that...

"Besides," Grandpa Angus added, lighting a small fire of suspense within my being, "he and I have a lot of catching up to do."

* * *

If my mom knew – if she ever knew – what happened after she walked out that door, she probably would have screamed so loud that the action would cause her to faint.

For the first time in my life, on that night, it occurred to me that Grandpa Angus was very possibly crazy. For a long time, I'd perceived him as strong. Wise. Perceptive. Authoritative. But never before had madness entered the picture. Yeah, he'd drop an eccentric joke here or there, but nothing to make you think the guy was bonkers.

Then came the rooftop.

Angus had a pretty big house, approaching 5,000 square feet. He'd made his living for years as a carpenter, and then later as a supervisor of other carpenters. Big contracts, major jobs. I'd always had the sense my dad was intimidated by the older man's earning power – a considerable thing to behold, seeing as my dad was hardly a slouch in that department. Indeed, had it not been for my father's togetherness, I'd have never squeezed my wheelchair through our front door.

Anyway, a particular point of pride for Grandpa Angus was his roof. It was flat as a board yet made of stone. Not concrete – actual carved rocks. Grandpa hadn't been kidding around. His rooftop was like a patio, only bigger, and without any adjoining structure as its backdrop.

And that's where he took me like five minutes after she left.

It wasn't easy. He'd built a fine wood staircase leading up to the roof – kind of like the classiest fire escape you'd ever seen – but just 'cause we weren't going up a ladder didn't mean this was child's play.

No – he actually draped me over his shoulder. It felt silly for a moment – now I REALLY felt like a kid – but any sense of levity vanished as I processed the possibility that he could *drop* me.

Great. Imagine how wondrous that would be:

"Sorry, guys. The last time I had your kid in my care, I shot him. And this time, well, I dropped him down the steps!"

Only, it was only funny in theory.

As he lowered my body to that polished stone roof, he let out a grunt that could have cut right through my grandma's medicated sleep. Then he vanished for a little while, the kind that flirts with becoming a long while until it gets mercifully interrupted – in this case by the sound of him banging my chair up those steps.

I didn't even want to think about getting back down.

He helped me into the chair. "You okay?"

"Yeah."

Truth was, I was. He'd taken a monumental task and downsized it to a trivial errand. Behind me, I heard the sound of scraping. It was Grandpa Angus pulling a chair in my direction. When he arrived, he positioned his chair so it was both beside and facing mine. For a moment, I tensed at the thought of an inane, heavy-eye-contact discussion, but prior to taking a seat, he stood behind me and turned my chair around...

To face the view.

Oh man – I wish words existed to describe that view. The way the stars looked, it was as though the angels were up there having a light-weaving competition. In an instant, the mere sight filled me with...well, hope. Or at least something resembling it.

Perspective?

Calmness?

I got injected with a sterling reminder that I was part of something much greater and grander than I was. Just a speck inside this massive universe. Experiencing existence like countless other living beings, complete with thoughts, perceptions, and feelings.

But no worse or no better than anyone, or anything, around me – now or in times past or in times to come.

We weren't even talking yet, but the sky was speaking volumes.

Angus settled down beside me. Yet again, the man didn't let me down. No way he'd have brought me up here just to chat face-to-face. No, the view was a third string in our conversation, and in its own way, it was the loudest.

"Beautiful night," he said.

"It really is."

"I'm haunted by what I did," he said.

My breathing changed. Eyes blinked – and my eyelashes felt a little moist. I wasn't anywhere near "crying" territory, yet he'd certainly warmed up my emotional grid.

What was I going to say? That it was "okay"? Because THAT certainly wasn't true. Right at that moment, I resented my state more than ever.

Not because of what the old man had said.

But because I wanted to get up and run away.

Not an option. There we were. Thankfully, momentarily, he saved me the trouble of replying:

"I don't sleep; you know that. I feel like...a failure.

"And I'm not asking for forgiveness."

"I do forgive you," I said. It was beyond awkward. We weren't built for these depths. Our relationship was supposed to coast along on outward simplicity. But not anymore, I suppose...

"Well, I thank you for that, Tucker. But you're a man. And a man has struggles in his life. And you, kid – you've got a lot of life left to cover. And in that life, there'll be crappy days. Plenty of 'em. I don't have to tell you that. And I want you to know that as those days come, you have my permission to pour your hate into me.

"Just: Use it. Use me. Use what I did...for the sake of getting that darkness out of your heart. I won't be here much longer. A decade if I'm lucky. So what I'm saying will largely apply after I'm gone. You may love me, Tucker, and I know you do, but you're only human, so when those days come...I'm here. Whether that means calling and yelling...or just waving your fist up at heaven and screaming my name."

"Assuming you don't go to Hell," I said.

Silence. We heard some crickets far away. Then the two of us broke into a *ridiculous* laugh. I mean, it went on and on. I really did get worried about waking Grandma at that point, along with some of the neighbors. But whatever:

We couldn't help ourselves.

How badly we'd needed some lightness in between us.

"Want to hear something strange?" I asked.

"Go. Sure."

"I'm not angry at you at all."

"Well, I appreciate you saying that."

"It's not just something I'm saying. It was an accident. We're lucky I'm alive. But the twisted thing is – and please don't tell my mom this..."

I had a feeling he knew precisely where this was going...

"...I'm pissed off at my dad. Like, a lot of the time. We just don't click. And lately, with my situation, he gets under my skin more than ever."

"Mmm," he said. Even though we'd established that this was a private conversation, Grandpa was too smart and classy to say anything negative about my dad, even if only to prevent me from having another reason to be annoyed with him. Finally, after a few slow moments, he said, "Your dad has a lot to prove, you know?"

"How so?"

Grandpa Angus angled his body more toward mine, making himself a bit diagonal and putting us out of strict alignment. "From the day I met him, long ago, I could tell within moments he was a very smart guy. Not smart like you or me; we're more philosophical. Your dad's more grounded. He operates well in the world. Makes a good living. Takes care of business. Good husband. Nice guy – very nice guy."

I got the slightly sticky feeling that Grandpa Angus – never one to try too hard – was doing exactly that. On the other hand, it came as a relief to me that I couldn't sincerely disagree with a word he said.

"But – and I swear to you, Tucker, this is the truth – within minutes, maybe even moments, I had the thought that his intelligence was possibly doing him more harm than good. 'Cause he's a sensitive man, your father. He picks up things. And those things have a way of getting stuck on him. So you get drinking. You get fighting. You get...some trouble out of the deal."

"I'm like that, too," I said. The words were quiet.

He looked at me. "I know you are, kid."

I looked back at him. "It's light and dark. We all

have a mixture, I guess..."

"Ain't that the truth?"

"And I see him, and it's like I'm seeing my own darkness. Only on the outside. A version of myself, maybe one that's scared, or uptight. Afraid of being weak.

"And sometimes...this thought occurs to me. About being in this chair. Sometimes it's like...and I don't fully mean this...but sometimes it's like maybe I'm better off, you know? Maybe if I had things my way, and could roam wherever I wanted to...

"I'd be like him."

Again, the night sounds filled the gap in our conversation.

"There are far worse things to be, Tucker."

"I know."

"And few better things to aspire to."

"I know."

We kept our eye contact fixed. Then it happened: The tears came. Not from him – from me. I felt so typical, sitting there crying; it was too predictable a factor in this conversation. He'd already provided the suspenseful teaser, then he'd gone to the trouble of carrying me up here, and now here I was, right on cue, having an emotional moment.

Yet the moment wasn't going away.

"Will he be OK, you think? My dad?"

"Oh, sure. These things happen. We like to think they happen to other people, far away, but that's just a lie we tell ourselves. Same lie I told myself the night before that gun went off. That the pain's far away. That it doesn't apply here.

"But it does. And then what? People have choices. All kinds of 'em, naturally. But in the end, most choices come down to the big one."

"Which is what?"

"Life versus death." He hadn't missed a beat. It had been right there on the tip of his tongue. "Either you're gravitating toward one or the other. Each person, anywhere on Earth. Your dad; he gravitates toward life. I know him; I've seen the man. So for my money? He prevails."

"Pretty fitting since you just gave him your money."

We laughed again. This one wasn't as long or as hard, but just the same it was nice to experience.

"As for you, Tucker: You gravitate there, too. Toward life. Every day. Always have. Which is why, I think, the universe tested you this way. Someone up there knew you were up for this. It's one hell of a test. I don't know if I could do it..."

"But you're being tested, too, Grandpa. And I honestly don't know if I could trade my test for yours."

He nodded. Looked on back at the stars. When he looked back at me, I didn't meet his gaze. I was too busy blinking away my own tears.

"I'm gravitating toward life, too, Tucker. It's a conscious decision. Each and every day. I have to say it to myself. Out loud. Sometimes a hundred times a day!"

We laughed.

He went on, "But this life – what I have left of it – has to be a life. I know that much. Not just a crawl toward death."

Again, we looked up at the stars. Doing so gave me a chance not only to continue soaking up their beauty, but to soak in all the words that he'd said. That I'd said, too.

The whole exchange.

I kept on repeating it, in my head.

And I'd do so for the rest of my life.

CHAPTER 8

Racing

R ebecca was good throughout the day, but as the afternoon wore on, things started getting a little tense...

We were at a gym that Kip had partial ownership of. In the back was a large room with a wood floor that he used for murderball practice. The floor wasn't up to regulation standards, so he told me and the other three players to be hush-hush about the whole thing, but to be honest I had an easier time there than I had up at his place. Maybe 'cause I was more experienced by then. Or maybe 'cause I was surrounded by other players who were in the same boat as I was.

Two girls and one guy. All with spinal cord injuries. The oldest couldn't have been more than 30. Kip introduced us all, and I expected him to launch into one of those embarrassing segments where we all sat around in a circle and talked about ourselves and where we were from – along with the precise nature of our injuries – but I guess Kip knew that would have been irritating, 'cause he just went straight into practice.

I hardly even caught their names.

It was kind of like playing in a band, I guess. We communicated more with our chairs, our instincts, and our ball than we did through words or other ordinary bonding tools. The same way I imagined players in a band bonded mainly through their instruments.

It was hard for me to get a sense of whether I was good or not. After half an hour or so, I stopped even judging my performance in terms of good or bad. I just needed to get the ball over that line. Rarely did I manage to. Once I did, then another time I was like a foot away, but for the most part I found myself getting crushed by my opponents' chairs.

Which was fine by me, 'cause I was doing no small amount of crushing on my own.

It was fun. Kip had loaded up our chairs with fortifications before practice started – miniature bumpers and curved sheets of steel that looked like medieval shields – so even though it seemed like I was about to get really hurt at about 100 points, I didn't even come close. Once I realized I wasn't genuinely in harm's way – save for Kip's repeated advisement about watching our hands and fingers – I started to get a kind of rush. Like I was invincible.

Like, whether I had mad skill or no skill, I was a legitimate murderball player.

That was the most important part of that day, be it by Kip's design or by my own interpretation: The sense that I now understand the game from the inside, not just in terms of its rules and objectives, but as a cultural thing. A way of life.

A thing that's well worth doing.

February 1 was now two weeks away. We practiced on Saturdays, and two Saturdays from this one would be the big game. And although Kip tossed in a bunch of words about wanting to win and crush the other team, the truth was I think he just wanted us to have fun. Or at least that was my personal takeaway.

Which was fine by me since, being paralyzed people, society didn't generally think to issue us fun experiences as a matter of course.

* * *

The problems with Rebecca had started almost right away, however.

Although she was cool for most of the training session, from the moment we walked in she was a source of issues. Namely: She was the only non-murderball party in attendance.

Nobody else had brought along a companion.

For half a second, this made me feel cool, emphasizing the fact that I alone might have had ample game to bring a companion. But right after that wave of confidence passed, I got self-conscious that the move was obnoxious. That maybe the other players wouldn't have wanted to feel judged.

That maybe Kip, likewise, would have preferred a closed session.

But nobody said anything, so she sat where girlfriends generally sit at things like those: on the sidelines. Once in a while, I heard her cheer. I loved that she did, particularly since it was out of alignment with her overall shy nature, but my reactions were mixed with that fear of being judged.

Anyway: The practice was over in a snap. It had been slated for two hours, but chop off the half an hour spent fortifying our chairs and you had a lean 90 minutes out there on the wood. It went by fast.

I could have stood for more.

But apparently Kip had other things in mind:

"Okay," he said, stepping forward and clapping his hands, "anybody got plans?"

Bunch of no's and shrugs came from the group (the latter for those whose bodies still allowed for shrugging). Only Rebecca withheld a reply.

"'Cause if you want, you all are invited to see me race. I'm doing a charity event, half an hour from here. Anybody without a ride, you're welcome in my van. Free passes all around, which gets you a drink and a snack from concessions."

I was in. I didn't even look at Rebecca. I said it sounded awesome, as did my trio of murderball companions.

But right away, I sensed that vibe pouring off Rebecca's being.

The one that told me I'd just made a big mistake.

* * *

"This sucks," she said.

She was behind the wheel. I was riding shotgun, my chair crammed, folded, in the back. Her car's trunk was too small to accommodate it, but it fit in the backseat within an inch of its life.

"Whoa," I replied. "Why are you being so harsh?"

"We were supposed to have dinner."

"We can have dinner at the race."

"We can get snacks at the race. All junk food."

"I can buy you dinner at the race!" I exclaimed, not with anger, just total mystification over the fact that she deemed this worthy of discussion.

"That's not the point!"

"What is the point then??"

But I already knew the point. Obviously, she wanted me to herself. A break from the scene. No more Kip for a while. She'd put in her time back at the gym, and now it was time for some intimacy – or relative privacy, at least.

And I understood. I felt bad about agreeing for us both; it was kind of on the patriarchal side. But on the other hand, she had to understand a few things:

"Kip's important to me," I said.

"I hope I'm important to you, too!"

"Duh! I'm not talking about, like, Kip as a person..." (Even though I was.) "...I'm talking about the whole thing. Murderball. Being in this world. It's giving me life."

"I give you life, too, I hope."

"It's not a competition."

"Sure feels like one."

"Rebecca!" I had to gather my breath. "I need as much...life...as I can get right now, okay? All available sources. I'm kind of hanging by a thread here."

"But we're a unit, Tucker. We come as a pair, okay?"

"Okay."

"So you can't just answer for me without asking."

"I get it. I'm sorry." Then, the kicker, which bore zero sincerity: "We don't have to go."

But that was a bluff, plain and simple. Had she decided we weren't going right then and there, the end of our relationship wouldn't be too far around the corner. How lame would that be, to commit and then bail? I'd have to make up some lie to tell Kip, which I hated doing, 'cause then I'd somehow end up being caught down the road. Already, I was buckling under the negative possibilities of not showing up. But:

"It's okay. We can go. But just know for next time."

"I will. I do. And thank you."

I tilted my head toward the window and smiled victoriously.

Then off we went.

* * *

I couldn't believe it was only my second time watching Kip race.

The guy had occupied so much space in my mind, and then my schedule, that it seemed as though I'd been to 100 of his races. Right away, the scene got its hooks in me: the crazy sound of the engines, the hot blue electricity in the air, the shared anticipation of the crowd.

All so tangible.

All so deep.

Although my body couldn't feel below my neck – save for my arms, of course – being at these races presented some approximation of overall physical sensation. As did playing murderball.

And having sex.

This was key, the direction my life was going in. Although on some level things were a mess – the fact that Rebecca spent so much time under my skin; the fact that my dad had a court arraignment scheduled in one month's time; the fact that my grandfather, though we'd made our peace, was now getting three hours of sleep per night – the good news was I was gathering experiences and sides of reality that returned me to a state of full engagement.

Not even returned, really. 'Cause so much of this stuff was new.

It would have been so easy to wither following my accident. Had my personality been even 1 percent different, I might have spent all my time cooped up in my bedroom, staring at the wall. But it seemed like the universe, and/or God, was tossing opportunities in my direction. It was my job, then, to catch them, as best I could.

Lean toward life, like Angus had put it.

I was leaning as hard as I could.

Each day, every day, at the center of my sights was that sense of normalcy. Would it ever come? Would I ever feel that click? Maybe a certificate would arrive in the mail, alerting me to the fact that I'd graduated into a state of normalcy.

It was fun to picture, albeit stupid.

'Cause that for me was the ultimate prize right then.

Unfortunately, however, as we sat in the stands, right there at the front, by the partition between the crowd and the track, my murderball teammates in a line at our side, Rebecca gave me far more normalcy than I could stand...

* * *

"It's loud!" she yelled.

"What?!"

"LOUD!"

"I know! The engines are sick!"

"I'm getting nauseous!"

"You're what??" (The truth was I'd heard that one just fine.)

"Nausea..." She pointed at her throat and chest. "Like I'm gonna puke."

"You're fine. Take a deep breath!"

She got up and left. I blinked after her, craning my head to follow her trajectory, but within a moment the colors and arches of the crowd had devoured her.

Something resembling panic gripped me. The thought of one of my "guardians" not being 100 percent had never crossed my mind. Even when Angus had hauled me up those steps, I was more worried about getting dropped or my mom finding out than I was about him potentially breaking his neck or having a sudden heart attack.

Was she coming back?

I was freaking a little. If she was sick, I'd have to look after her. No big deal, that – but then again I wasn't the most mobile human being on Earth.

In fact, in our little group, the most mobile human was the one out there racing on the orange motorbike. So good luck getting *his* help for the next couple hours!

I wheeled my chair back from the partition, then curved a little to my left, intent upon turning it around

– but then I stopped.

The crowd was too thick. I couldn't navigate this all by myself. And even if I made it over to the restrooms, unless I managed to connect with her again, I ran the risk of having to return to my seat all alone.

No good. I couldn't be wheeling around asking every single person to move. And I could only imagine all the concerned Good Samaritans who'd start asking if I was okay and then offering help.

So I realigned my chair's wheels and rode forward, bumping the partition and staying still. Sure, it would have been the heroic move to go and wait for her, but had she suddenly bailed on me, it would have been the height of foolish.

And that possibility – the one of her bailing, the one where she was now in her car driving home – was what overtook my mind as I sat there pretending to watch the race. Every so often, the crowd would cheer, but half the time I had no clue what they were reacting to. I kept running calculations through my mind: Was she really that pissed at me? Was she really not feeling well? Had she secretly been as annoyed with me as I was with her?

No – stop being ridiculous, Tucker.

I was reverting back to my old self, the one who'd existed before we got together. Only this time it wasn't about scoring the girl; this time it was actually about still having a ride back home.

And that's when I realized that Rebecca and I had

a problem.

It went beyond her simply being annoying. It went deeper than me wanting to explore other options. It was becoming a simple matter of me not feeling that attached to her anymore. If the possibility of her dumping me was ranked lower than the possibility of her not giving me a ride on my list of priorities, then we certainly had an issue on our hands.

I kept waiting. Fake-watched the race. It was starting to seem like a really long time. First 15 minutes passed. Then 20. When 20 made way for 25, my concern transitioned from theoretical and neurotic to warranted and tangible.

Where was she, already?

That was it; I couldn't take this. I had to go and find out. Even if it meant not getting back to my seat. Or if it meant tolerating the charity of some stranger to get back. No way I could sit there in that state. And besides, when she found out I'd gone to find her, she'd no doubt be flattered, which would be good for us.

Which of course tested the meaning of "good."

But still: I rolled. It took work, given the thickness of the crowd. I was on a flat surface, but well below the eye-lines of most people in my way. That meant that with one person after another, I'd have to vocally make my presence known.

Invariably, as they looked down, they bounced out of the way like I could set them on fire. Distant looks. Frightened looks. Looks of naked alarm.

This was exactly why it had taken me this long to move.

Meanwhile, I had to admit to myself that Rebecca represented more than just a ride: She made me look good. With her pushing me, I would have been a stronger package. Still, the vacant stares and sneers would come, but at least I'd be in the company of a legitimate beauty. Now, I was just some dude in a wheelchair.

By the time I reached the restrooms, it felt like a million years had gone by.

I saw a long line stretching into each. Rebecca was nowhere in sight. But if she'd waited on one of those lines, 25 minutes wasn't even very long. My throat clenched at the thought of her puking in a stadium toilet. Not the most sanitized environment on Earth.

As I waited, I started to cool off inside. It felt good to have done the right thing by following her. And although it may have been too late, I got concerned about her not feeling well. Naturally, I'd do whatever it took to get us home, no matter how much of a pain that would mean for Kip or whoever else drove us.

But as five more minutes clicked on by, I started to re-experience that sinking feeling that perhaps I'd be begging for a ride not for two...but for one.

"Come on, Becky," I said under my breath.

No idea why I'd called her Becky. It seemed to mesh with the newness of my surroundings, and the novelty of this particular experience.

I looked around. This was feeling steep. I was out here now all by myself. For the first time since that gun had fired, I was acutely aware of how much help I needed to get by. Nothing like being in a crowd this big to make you feel alone.

And nothing like the presence of a thousand total strangers to make you cherish the people that you know.

When she saw me, she smiled.

I smiled back. There she was: my dream. Looking a few too many shades of pale, but still a sight of beauty regardless.

"Are you okay?"

She hovered over me. "You came over here?"

"Yeah. Somehow."

We laughed. She said, "I had dry heaves. Didn't puke."

"Ah, man. Long day."

"I know."

"Should we go home?"

She fished her phone from her pocket and lit up the screen. "Still got another hour here."

"Yeah, but if you don't feel good..."

"But you gotta say goodbye to Kip."

"I'll say you didn't feel good. He's got like 10 million fans. He'll get over it."

She smiled, but circled around my chair. "No," she said, behind me, yes, but oh-so-close. "Let's watch the rest. I'm fine."

* * *

The trip back to our seats was the opposite of my solo trip to the bathroom.

Never before had the difference between being alone and having company seem so stark. I remembered Jordan once talking about marketing. He'd taken a couple of classes in college. He once told me about something called "social proof", which is the idea that you trust somebody more when you know somebody they know. Reason being, the person in common lends the would-be stranger credibility. That's why well-known actors and personalities are more popular in movies and on TV than relative unknowns. We've seen their stuff; we feel more comfortable.

And in the absence of a *known* entity, Jordan had said, a *fellow* entity was the next best thing.

In other words, although the ideal social proof is a familiar party, any party at all is better than none at all. As a solo act, therefore, I didn't inspire people's confidence. With Rebecca at my back, however (literally: she had my back), I was perceived as an entirely different being.

This didn't even have so much to do with my position in a wheelchair. For all people, at all levels of society, it applied. A guy with a wife registers differently from a guy without one. Two bodies coming down a dark alleyway are far less threatening than one – even though two are physically stronger.

ROLLING HOME

So I valued Rebecca – treasured her, in fact – but I had some heavy lifting to do in terms of how much that value was tied to her usefulness and how much was tied to our authentic closeness.

For now, however, I couldn't sort that out.

It was time to return to watching the race.

Unfortunately, though, that spectacle was over in about two minutes...

* * *

Rebecca's hand was wrapped around mine.

It was her way of telling me things were fine; a way of making peace without having to talk the entire day to death. Fine by me: I was grateful for the contact.

And it was fitting to have contact with her when Kip's bike flipped over.

* * *

We knew it would happen before it did.

A woman was running out there on the track. Large woman, wide at the hips, with over-sized blue jeans on. Right away, the mere sight of her brought the crowd to its feet. Not with excitement, but with collective alarm.

Why was that woman out there on the track?

The answer was visible to Rebecca before it was to me. It was a little black speck, blurring along on the dirt.

The lady's poor dog, which we'd later learn had jumped out of her hands.

On instinct, the woman ran after her puppy, fearing that it was about to get hurt. But the animal lived, made it clean to the grass taking up the track's center.

The lady, amazingly, survived as well.

But Kip Cruiser swerved out of the way, and in the process hit a barricade, which sent his bike – and his body – into a triple, upward-flying cartwheel.

* * *

Chaos erupted.

Myself and my three fellow murderball players were the only ones in the stadium that weren't on our feet. A panic like nothing I'd ever known overtook my being. It was like at that moment – at the risk of sounding corny – Kip and I were a single person.

His pain was my pain.

His accident was my accident.

I'm not saying this due to the connection we shared as people. I'm saying that ever since that bullet had left that gun, this was the single largest shock I'd endured. And the factors were identical:

Wondering how bad the damage was.

Wondering how close death was.

Wondering what reality would serve up in just another minute, another second, another moment...

ROLLING HOME

Even though we had come in with Kip, we were now being told by security to leave. The whole crowd was being asked to disperse. As we did so, we were not unlike cows being herded: heads hung low, spirits damp. No one felt cheated out of the remainder of the show. Everyone was too nervous about the status of its star.

And as rampant as the fear were the rumors.

Left and right, you had people saying they'd heard he was dead. Others muttered that he was alive yet paralyzed. I wondered how in the world such information could have reached their possession. As Rebecca wheeled me toward the main exit, she fired up her phone and handed it to me. Told me to search the news, see if anything was there.

Ironic, to be turning to the Internet for info about a guy who was merely a few hundred yards away from me.

News had indeed traveled fast. Video uploads of the crash were running. But I had no desire to see that site ever again.

Most news sources repeated the same pair of grim words: "critical condition."

Followed by the promise that more information was soon to come.

I turned off the phone and handed it back to Rebecca. If he died, I didn't want to read about it. That was the least God could do for me at this juncture.

"Let's go to the hospital," I said.

"Which hospital?" she asked.

"It's gotta be Cathedral's. That's the closest one."

"What if they're taking him somewhere else?"

"Well let's check there first." I was snapping at her, and fortunately for my sake she aired no objection. "And if it's not the one, we'll call around."

She wheeled me onward, toward her car. But we had a logistical matter to take care of prior to taking off: namely the other three people who couldn't drive.

The location of Kip's van was now unknown, and even if it wasn't, that wouldn't matter very much without the keys and a driver. So Jared, the oldest in the group, hopped on his own mobile and arranged for a shuttle service. Not wanting to be rude to them, Rebecca and I hung around 'til their own ride showed.

Even though doing so chewed away at my nerves.

Every two seconds or so, I wanted to leap back on Rebecca's phone. I had one, too, of course, but hers got faster Internet service. If Kip was gone, I wanted to know.

But each time I thought to look up the news, I reminded myself that it'd be better to hear it straight from the source.

Thirty minutes went by before the shuttle showed. As a courtesy, Jared offered me a ride in it, but we all knew full well that I was sticking with Rebecca. I thanked him anyway. They asked me to promise to text them when I got any news. We all exchanged numbers and I pledged to make it so.

ROLLING HOME

* * *

Cathedral's was indeed the hospital, and that turned out to be a lucky thing for Kip, as it was a nice place, first-rate, bearing more of a resemblance to a five-star hotel than a hospital. That was the good news. The bad news was, the hospital couldn't tell us much. He was still alive, which was good news, but they wouldn't say in what condition, much less how bad.

We sat in the waiting room.

"You okay?" I asked Rebecca. "This could be a while."

"I'm okay. I'm here."

I looked around. Before my brain could even fully fire the expectation of this occurring, a nearby bank of elevators chimed and Monica, wearing sunglasses and by herself, stepped out. My neck stretched upward. I'd half – or less than half – foreseen her appearance, just the way it had happened. Not like in a psychic sense, just in the sense that she was an inevitable factor in this emergency.

And here she was.

She didn't take notice of me. Part of me worried that I'd have to reintroduce myself. Prior to her taking a seat, she had a tense exchange with the reception staff. She received the same exact upload as we had: critical condition; they're working hard; please, just, have a seat.

It was maddening.

When Monica came over, I gave her a wave. Part of me wanted to remain aloof, the better to give her the space she needed, but by then I was an expert on social etiquette when it came to traumatic situations. No way was I about to risk being the loser who sits there quietly.

"Hi, Tucker." She actually managed a smile.

"Hey, Monica. This is Rebecca."

"Hi, Rebecca." They shook hands, then Monica sat right across from us, a welcome sign that our presence was more welcome than not.

Also in attendance, some 20 feet away, their bright orange jackets soaking up the light, was Kip's racing crew, but I had no notion of interacting with them. And neither, it seemed, as the moments ticked by, did Monica. As to whether that was an extension of her disapproval of his racing or just a measure of her not knowing those guys very well, I couldn't be sure.

"So this sucks," I said, by way of breaking the ice.

"I should've expected it," Monica replied, her neck tense as she shook her head. "I've been telling him to cool it lately. He didn't even have to do tonight's. It was practically a favor, the money they gave him."

I swallowed. Everybody's human tragedy is a thing of layers. It's not just tragic on a single layer – no. The tragedy seeps down to different areas. Like with me, it wasn't only about me being paralyzed. It was also about my grandpa having pulled the trigger. And the fact that we'd been out on what was supposed to have been a fun, spirited outing. And the fact that I was so young. And the mishap with the gun holster.

Yeah, tragedy just has a way of expanding...

Now with Kip, it wasn't as simple as a guy getting wrecked on a bike. You had his girlfriend's objection to him biking at all. You had the fact that him being on a bike was his calling. You had the sheer, spontaneous stupidity of that dog running onto the track, and the understandable yet terrible choice by his owner to follow.

As to what else was coming, we could only brace ourselves.

But one thing was for certain: At times like these, the badness spread itself out and made itself comforting.

The goodness, on the other hand, you had to look for.

* * *

Broken hip.

That was the long and short of it.

Other minor injuries dotted Kip's body, and he'd been admitted to the hospital with some tell-tale signs of brain injury, but a thorough examination of his brain, complete with the fact that he woke up after a couple of hours, allowed the doctors to pin the worst of it on his hip damage.

It was a resounding relief.

Monica started to cry. I, too, had tears dangling from the fronts of my eyes. As for Rebecca, by then she was fast asleep, her cheek bunched up against my shoulder. I patted her, waking her, and said, "He's fine. He's gonna make it."

She sprung upright, blinking. Looked around. Saw Monica dabbing her eyes with Kleenex, and thanking the doctor who'd stepped forward with the news. Rebecca, likewise, tossed him a "Thank you", but at that moment she seemed more asleep than awake.

"When can we talk to him?" Monica asked.

I liked that: her use of the word "we." It made me feel like I was part of their posse.

"Just a few more minutes," the doctor said. "We're wheeling him out to change rooms."

* * *

The amazing thing about Kip Cruiser was, when they wheeled him out on a bed toward his new room, he still – despite being on his back, despite his face being puffy and inflamed, despite his eyes being only partially open – had that ridiculously inspiring glow about him.

Or maybe I was just so happy to see him.

Monica certainly was, as well. She raced over to him, poured herself onto him. He hooked a weak arm around her back and rubbed it. "Jeez, some points in your column, huh?" he said. "Now you got ammo when we argue about racing."

She stood upright, tracking the bed as the orderlies pushed it. "Yeah, right. Like I'd ever want this to happen."

"I know, I know, I'm kidding, I'm kidding. Hey, sport."

Those words were aimed at me.

"Hey, buddy. You gave us a good scare."

The racing crew was gathering, too. Lots of chatter, verging on commotion. Kip's body was taking in lots of pats, kisses, and hugs.

The moment, no question about it, was joyous.

But when we at last got to Kip's room, he'd bring the pain.

* * *

"No more racing," he said.

By then, it was only me, Rebecca, and Monica on hand. The crew had taken off to give Kip his privacy, and we were just about to, also, but Kip had raised a hand and asked us to stay a minute.

For he'd had something important to share.

And that thing turned out to be the end of his career.

"Are you serious?" Monica asked. To her credit, if my intuition meant anything, she sounded way more upset than relieved.

"Dead serious. No pun intended."

I cracked half a smile, but still: This was terrible news. Sure, the fates had made Kip's decision for him, but certainly well before he'd been ready to throw in the towel.

"How do you know?" Monica asked.

He shrugged. "Hip's a piece of crap. It's shattered. They're gonna replace it. And I'll have physical therapy. But no way in the world it'll ever be what it was."

"You don't know that," Monica said.

This, to me, was what true love looked like: Despite her own self-interest, she was on his side.

"I do," he said. "I asked the doc. He's on my side. More or less."

"Your *side*?" she asked. "Is this something you want??"

"Look: He wants me to stay positive. He thinks I can get maximum mobility back. But when pressed, he admitted some skepticism as to whether that mobility would be the equal of being a champion bike racer. And I don't want to go back out there just to be mediocre and get people's sympathy. In a way, it's a blessing. I'll go out strong."

This guy was, by then, my biggest hero. He'd just hours earlier weathered what had possibly been the biggest storm of his lifetime, he was no doubt enduring unimaginable pain despite the meds they had him on, and there he was, calmly declaring that his dream, his love, his great life calling...was coming to an end.

I couldn't believe it.

"Let me text the others," I said, digging out my phone and getting buried in it. Although I'd known precisely how to handle Monica back in the waiting room, right now I was truly at a loss for words. The part of me that wanted to insist that he'd race again someday was in a deep, thick battle with the part that loved how easily he was moving on.

I sent out the word. Within moments, the chimes of relief came in. I repeated what the murderball guys had to say: all good words, wishing Kip the best.

Then finally, not wanting to go down as the guy who'd had nothing to say about Kip's big announcement, I dove in and addressed it:

"Well, I think you're an inspiration," I said.

He and Monica and Rebecca all looked my way.

"Like you said," I went on, "you go out on top. And jeez, man, the grace with which you're doing it. I don't think I would be that relaxed."

He smiled at me, pointed a finger my way. "You, my friend, are the inspiration."

"Ah, get out of here with that."

"It's true. You and guys like you."

"Now you're just trading one compliment for another..."

"Not for a second, buddy. I'm lucky to know you. I consider it a blessing to know anyone who's strong enough to survive a blow like the one you took.

"'Cause when I survive my own blows, I can look to your example, and see exactly how I should handle it."

* * *

It meant the world to me.

All in all, tragedy aside, this had turned into one heck of a good night. I flashed back briefly to the moment when Rebecca and I had fought about coming, and thanked my lucky stars that she'd gone my way.

As for Rebecca, well...as much as she was happy that Kip was OK, and as good as it was for the two of us that we'd managed to make our peace, I think in the end she would regret being present on that night.

Because that also turned out to be the night when we met Brianna.

* * *

She was Monica's best friend.

She was walking in as we were (finally) getting ready to jet. But as it turned out, you couldn't just take off like a second after meeting Brianna, 'cause she was something of a Chatty Cathy – in the best possible way.

Extroverted. Warm. Carried the conversation.

And had such striking physical beauty, that in truth, I could have stayed for another few hours.

Kip was sharp, painkillers or otherwise, and he alone detected my attraction to Brianna. I don't even think Rebecca caught it, for despite the fact that Brianna's beauty was self-evident, we were, after all, still in a hospital.

And I was, after all, still a guy in a wheelchair.

But right away, I kind of got a vibe from Brianna. There may have been five of us in that room, but as far as I was concerned it was just her and me.

We certainly had plenty to talk about. I recalled the accident. Then the aftermath, both online and off. Brianna said she'd been in a movie when it happened, then almost neglected to turn her phone back on afterward, in which case she would have gone home and fallen asleep.

Fortunately for me – I mean, Monica and Kip! – she'd managed to make it.

Another interesting detail of Brianna's story was who she had been at the movie with. Guy named Mike, apparently. She complained about him. Said he was all macho. Tried too hard.

I remembered what Kip had told me about what women need most:

Feeling safe, and being with a guy who was vulnerable.

Here I am, I said to Brianna.

But at that point I was only talking with my eyes.

* * *

The car ride home with Rebecca was chatty, also.

We still had lots of adrenaline in us based on all

we'd gone through. And we knew that our sleep would be deep and perfect in light of the relative relief we'd gotten at the end.

"Do you think he's serious?" Rebecca asked.

"Who Kip? About what?"

"That he's okay with moving on. Maybe he's just relieved to be alive."

"Maybe. But I think what he told me was true."

"Which part?"

"About guys like me. Weathering the big storms. You put it into perspective, it's just bike riding."

"Yeah, but it was his profession. The thing he's famous for."

"Maybe there's more to life..."

"Maybe. But on some level, that's gotta hurt."

I looked out the window. I didn't want to get into it. She was right, of course – and he was only human – but at the moment I wasn't too keen on exploring the downsides of Kip's transition. More for me was admiring his enormous grace.

Along with the text message that he sent me.

"Who's that?" she asked.

I studied my phone. I cracked a smile. "Just Kip," I said.

"Saying goodnight," I lied.

For he hadn't texted me goodnight.

But he had texted me a pair of words: "You devil."

I turned my phone off and we rode on.

CHAPTER 9

Exploding

When February 1 finally came, it came gift-wrapped in a box of drama.

First was the morning, when I argued with my dad. It happened in the kitchen. The whole thing escalated so fast that my head could spin.

Bottom line: He was supposed to take me to my game. But he was backing out and putting the task on Jordan because – get this – he had an appointment with a psychologist.

"What?" I asked. "The judge is making you do this."

"What?" he echoed, his forehead muscles tightening. "No – I haven't even been arraigned yet, Tucker. That's in a week."

"Is that when they sentence you?"

"No!" His volume was loud enough to shake me – to even hint at tickling the parts of me that could no longer feel.

"Then what's going on? You knew about this game!"

"I know!"

"So you're seeing a shrink now?"

"Yes."

Jordan entered the room, scooping/scraping his keys up off the counter. "Let's go, Tuck. You're gonna be late."

"Have a good game." That was my dad's lame attempt at being supportive.

I wheeled right over to him, tempted to roll right onto his toes, but stopping short out of sheer civility. "You were supposed to take me."

"Jordan will take you."

"Come on, bro! We're late!"

"I don't care who DRIVES me. I'm talking about you being there. Watching me!"

I could see the naked pain in my dad's gaze. "Okay, I get it. And I'm sorry. But I'm struggling here, kid."

"And I'm not?? I should be the one in therapy!"

My dad circled behind me, took hold of my chair, and began to march it forward. "You get yours playing murderball; I get mine with a shrink."

"Bullshit!"

"Tucker!"

I reached out and hooked my hand into the chair of a table right beside the front door. The table scraped its way into a diagonal position. My dad had no choice but to stop. Once he did, I wheeled away from him and spun around to face him.

He looked...small, somehow. Like weak. Even childlike. As much as I would have liked to believe that I got this impression 'cause I was intimidating to him, the truth was I think he was going through his own personal Hell.

So maybe therapy was called for, then.

But not before I administered to him a taste of my own medicine:

"You're so thoughtless."

"Tucker!"

"You are, Dad. Like, what are you even gonna discuss with that therapist?"

"Things that you could not bear to hear."

"Oh yeah? Really, Dad? Tell me all about what I can't bear. Go 'head. 'Cause from where I'm *sitting,* it kind of seems like I handle a lot."

"Agreed!" His volume had just hit its maximum. "So handle this, then. I'm not coming to your stupid game."

He turned his back on me to walk away.

But I wouldn't let him. I actually did wheel into him this time. His right knee popped forward and he almost fell. I gasped with near-silent relief when he pressed a palm against the wall and caught himself. When he turned to face me again, his facial skin was bright red. Maybe 10 percent a blush – but the rest was rage.

"Don't you EVER do that again!" he roared.

"The game's not stupid!"

"Neither is my appointment!"

"I never said it was! But you said you were coming, which makes you a liar."

He threw his hands up, then hit a volume I'd never heard from him before: "Call it whatever you want, Tucker! I'll certainly have plenty to discuss with the therapist after this!"

"Good! Make me an appointment, too! I'll have lots to say!"

"Oh, I will! And I'll pay for it, too. Since I pay for every other thing around here."

"Right, 'cause you're such a big man, right? Such a big man."

"TUCKER!" That was Jordan yelling. He was by the front door, evidently shocked into silence for a stretch prior to interjecting again.

My dad got right in my face. For half a second, in one hand, he clenched my cheeks. It hurt a little. My gum line ached. But he wasn't impulsive enough to hang on for long. He just settled for keeping his face in mine – like, right in mine, maybe two inches away at most.

"One day you'll be a man, kid. And YOU'LL

ROLLING HOME

KNOW HOW IT FEELS!!!"

I felt his breath. I saw the inside of his mouth: tongue, tonsils, uvula.

Then, that time, he really did turn and walk away.

* * *

We were 10 minutes late for the game, but it turned out that was OK 'cause Kip had told us to get there 30 minutes early. Smart move; that guy was as sharp as ever. I guess he supposed, or knew, that the handicapped can always use some extra traveling time.

Little did he know the dysfunctional source of my own delay.

Right when I got there, however, more problems greeted me. They came in the form of Rebecca, whose presence in the locker room off the court initially seemed exciting – a sensation that lasted for well under three seconds.

Then my mind switched to various versions of: What in the world is she doing here?

She marched up to me. I saw her bottom teeth. That was a bad sign; it was something of an animal reflex she sprung into whenever she was livid.

Which seemed to constantly be the case these days.

"What's up?" I asked.

I was in my uniform: the classic Kip Cruiser orange. I also had a no end of cool fortifications around my chair. Mad Max himself would have looked at it in awe. So Rebecca certainly had plenty of cool new things to take notice of.

Yet she chose to harp on something else entirely:

"Why is *she* out there?"

"Who?" I was squawking.

"Brianna!"

"Who's Brianna?" I asked, looking around to confirm the fact that – thank God – we were alone in there.

And, of course, my question was wholly insincere. I knew exactly who Brianna was, and we both knew it.

"Oh, you mean Monica's friend?"

"You are so full of crap!"

"Ssshhh." Even though we were alone, it seemed reasonable to try and get her to cool her volume just a pinch. I mean, if for no other reason than to keep my nerves from getting all knotted up.

Which of course had already happened, many moments ago.

"What do you care if she's here?" I asked.

"Monica's not here!"

"So what? She's here for Kip, then!"

"Why would she be here for Kip? She's Monica's friend!"

"You are...acting...completely crazy right now."

"Oh, I don't think so, Tucker. And thanks a lot, also, 'cause she's sitting right next to me."

Great. There it was: the real reason why Rebecca had just gone off like a time bomb. Not only did she have to be in the same room as Brianna, she had to be wedged right up beside her.

I had to admit to myself that had I been on the opposite side of this scenario – had there been, for example, a guy with eyes for Rebecca – then I could certainly think of a lot more rosy scenarios than being forced to sit right next to that person for an afternoon.

On the other hand, I'm not sure I would have gone off like that. I mean: I was now about two minutes late to the court. It was awful. I couldn't think straight. Did she really have to get me right then and there?

It wasn't like I'd cheated on her or anything.

At least not yet.

I'm kidding! Yeah, the thought had crossed my mind. I'm only human, after all. But as far as I was concerned, Brianna wasn't much more than a hot, cool girl. Certainly not a friend. Definitely not a legitimate option.

"I have to play," I said, rolling forward, letting my elbow touch the front of Rebecca's shirt.

"All right, whatever..." She muttered.

"Yeah, thanks for the good luck!" I snapped.

And it came out raw. Like, hateful almost. I hadn't even laid on that much attitude with my dad.

But on the other hand, my words weren't only directed at her.

They were directed at him, too. And his stupid therapy session. And my stupid spinal cord.

And just about everything negative in this whole stupid world.

AUSTIN CHARTERS

* * *

The good news was, I took that rage with me out on the court.

Then and there, that day, I got why whoever had chosen to call it "murderball" had done so. This was a serious outlet for aggression.

To be honest, although I didn't let onto as much with Kip, I didn't even care whether or not I won.

I guess when life hurts you bad, you become less petty. Or at least I managed to veer in that direction. Win, lose – who cares? We're all mortal.

All timed to lose in the end.

Or at least, you know, shed our mortal coil.

So I didn't care one bit about the opposing team. Truth be told, I found it hard to hate my fellow wheelchair riders, even if their core objective was to slaughter me out there.

As far as I was concerned, we were all in this together.

I played like lightning that day. Or at least felt that way. The speed of the wood beneath my body; hurtling by in a pure, blended blur. And not only did I not care about winning, I didn't even care about getting hurt.

'Cause, let's be honest, here: How much more "hurt" could I get?

I'd already bore personal witness to Level 9.9 on the human hurt scale. No way was another tenth of a percent gonna make me go crying to my mama.

ROLLING HOME

Speaking of whom, she was at work. Which was why my father had been tasked with taking me. But of course, like everything else in his life, he'd screwed that up, so now I was as good as alone out there.

Though I had that face of his – a couple inches from mine – fresh and bright within my head.

And every time I swerved toward an opponent, every time I found my sweat-drenched arms grappling for that ball (which more often than not, just bounced out of my grip like a feather being grabbed by a cat), my dad was out there fueling my rage.

I guess, in truth, he was my opponent. Certainly more so than the strangers on the court.

Was this why people all around the world played sports? Forget being in a wheelchair: Did every competitive action have an invisible competitor somewhere behind it?

I wondered about that out there that day. Wondered about baseball players, football, basketball, golf, you name it. What were they playing for?

Who were they really playing against?

In my case, no opponent, not even that damn little bullet, came near my dad in terms of its might. Why? Did I hate him? Of course not. Not even close.

But he...just...got...so far...under my skin.

WHAM!

I bashed into a woman from the opposing team. It was the first time out there that I'd made contact with a girl. For a split second, I felt guilt about it – until she gave as good as she'd received--

CRACK!

I swore I was about to fall over. I was up on one wheel, amazed by gravity's ability to still keep the other one rolling on the ground.

Then, right there in front of me, was Marty.

Guy from my own team. Beard and glasses. No motion in his legs.

No motion in his spine.

And then, for an instant, he had no sight, as well.

'Cause Marty and I crashed into each other like a pair of comets colliding.

And I laughed. The laugh came from deep inside. Like as deep as my well of laughter reaches. Wherever my first laugh ever, as a baby, had come from, was the precise source of these current laughs.

They were crazy. Delirious.

And entirely innocent.

Which was ironic, of course, seeing as murderball was a pretty guilty thing.

SMASH!

I took another blow on my right side. The female again, the other team. This time gravity didn't have my back.

My chair hit the ground with the weight of a thousand nightmares.

I went sliding. It was only three or five feet or so, but the trip seemed long since I didn't know when it would end.

Yet when it did, I was still there.
Albeit sideways.
A metaphor for my entire existence:
Still here. Just a little bit bruised.

* * *

"TUCKER!"

For the first time that day, the voice that yelled my name wasn't charged with malice. On the contrary, Kip Cruiser was sounding a clear note of amazement.

He ran his hand through my sweaty hair. We were back in the locker room, the whole team, with Rebecca nowhere in sight – which was fine by me.

"But we lost," I told him, as he'd somehow failed to miss that bit of information.

"So what, man? You played like a team that's bound to win. Give it up."

He held his fist before me. I bumped mine into it. "Drinks," Kip said, "burgers, fries. Junk food. Who's coming??"

He didn't even have to ask. Everyone was right there with him.

"I can give people rides," a familiar voice said.

I turned. There she was: a ray of light. Brianna. Hadn't seen her since the hospital. Had thought of her, of course, on an hourly basis.

"Hey, Tucker."

My soul leaped upward. She remembered my

name!

"Hey, um..." Oh, come on, don't be a jerk. "...Brianna."

I looked at Kip. He looked back at me. It didn't take up the space of a whole second, but within that span of time he conveyed to me with his gaze that he'd seen exactly what I'd done right there. How I'd thought of being too cool for school for a second, then made the wiser decision and played it polite.

And if I was wrong, it didn't matter.

'Cause Kip Cruiser was and remained The Man.

* * *

More drama preceded our trip to dinner. Only this time it didn't come with any yelling or frowning. Rather, it came quietly.

Silently, even.

It came in the form of the fact that Rebecca had left.

"She didn't say she was sick or anything?" I asked Jordan.

Behind the wheel, he shook his head. "Nah, nothing like that. Nothing, even. Like, she just got up and walked away."

"You're kidding me!"

"Hand on a stack of bibles, bro."

I thought back to the game. For the first time, amid all my adrenaline and self-renewal, I realized something critical that had happened back there:

Rebecca, as I played, had been entirely silent.

But Brianna had been pretty loud.

Yeah – in fact, she'd even called my name once or twice. I felt ridiculous for having had a delayed reaction on that one. When she'd said it in the locker room, it had been a surprise, but it shouldn't have been.

'Cause she'd been cheering me on.

Her. Not Rebecca.

Mind you, however, that Rebecca was shy. Not everybody can be expected to cheer. That wasn't the point, though. The point was that not only was Brianna cheering, she was doing so right there at Rebecca's side.

Gosh, I despised Rebecca at that moment.

Here I'd just had a major experience – a breakthrough, even; found a whole new reason for living – and her gift to me surrounding it had been a fight and the decision to abandon me.

Never before had I felt such fury.

My dad and Rebecca went together as a pair. One bailed at the outset; the other near the end (according to Jordan's account; he'd said she was gone 10 minutes before the game was over). I got all self-conscious: Was it something about me?

No. Damn. Maybe they were both envious...

The craziest part was that my dad's behavior had far more logical underpinnings than Rebecca's. At least he had recently been in a fight and gotten arrested. That'll certainly distract a guy.

As for her, she couldn't possibly dignify such a move. She'd walked out on me just when I'd needed her the most.

And that, to me, much as it broke my heart, was an unforgivable offense.

* * *

I showed up at the Snack Shack expecting to be angry and inward the entire time, but as it happened, Brianna put a pretty tidy end to my bad mood.

She was right beside me. Her knee was touching mine. I tried to guess whether or not there was meaning behind that. After all, she knew full well that I couldn't feel her. Did that erase any chance of an intimate undertone? Or was it the opposite?

Did my lack of physical feeling simply make me easier to flirt with?

I couldn't tell. So all I did was talk. For a while, we talked mainly about me: my accident, my family, my first encounter with Kip, my path to murderball.

But I wasn't about to let that go on for too long. Much as I appreciated being asked so many questions, I was keen on the fact that conversations are always way better as two-way streets.

What I learned was, she was 19. She wasn't Monica's friend – at least not at first. She'd started off as Monica's intern. Monica was very involved in the business side of Kip's career, and Brianna had emailed her a resume offering help. To Brianna's surprise, Monica had gone for it, but the arrangement elapsed after two semesters, after which they continued as friends.

Now it all made sense: Of course she'd be at the game when Monica wasn't. Of course she'd be the only "friend" at the hospital. Her previous work arrangement had made that sort of behavior a matter of course. Where they went, she went. And although she was closer to Monica than to Kip, she'd been motivated to get into the internship on account of being a huge fan of Kip's.

Gosh, if only Rebecca could know all this. She'd certainly be a lot more grounded about the lady's presence.

As for me, I had to admit, I felt a wee bit disappointed.

'Cause up until I found out why Brianna had shown up absent Monica, I'd kind of been hoping that Brianna had shown up to see me.

* * *

In the end, almost like I'd manifested it to happen, the night worked out exactly as I'd hoped it would.

Which is to say: It ended up just being me and Brianna, at a park not far from where we'd had our snack.

We'd ended up at the snack shack for like three hours. The first couple flew by, then the third one consisted of everybody trying to agree on how to pay the check and where, if anywhere, they wanted to go next. Monica showed up, a factor which lent the strange sensation of me and Kip having our girls out on a double date.

But that was, of course, entirely wishful thinking. The truth was, for now, I was happy to call Brianna my friend.

She was the one I spoke to most. Eventually, Jordan eyed his phone and said he had to take off. "I have a date of my own," he whispered to me.

I wished him luck.

Obviously, his use of the words "of my own" indicated that he'd entirely picked up on the fact that I was into Brianna. Either that or he was just trying to make me feel better about Rebecca. In any case, he was gone from there inside of five minutes. It didn't take Brianna very long to volunteer to be the one to take me home.

Only home was not where she took me – at least not right away.

The park was a place I'd gone to my whole life: Residential Hills, it was called, and it not only had your basic kids' stuff – swings and slides and so on – but it had a series of cool bridges winding through it. So Brianna, be it by a conscious choice or just a spontaneous instinct, took me there and wheeled me over those bridges.

Mostly, though, it was the talking that soaked up our attention.

"So what do you want to do?" she asked me.

"What's that?" I said, though I'd heard her just fine and was stalling.

"With your life? After college."

"Well I still have another year of high school next year..."

"Yeah, but it'll go fast. College is almost done for me."

"You're only halfway there!"

"Ah, but the second half's already accelerating. I can feel it."

"So you first: What do you wanna do?"

"Well, the strange thing is, this morning before the game, I was talking with Kip about him really expanding with the murderball. Going pro. Maybe even establishing his own league. It's his primary focus right now. So maybe I'll go back with those guys, help them build that company."

I smiled. To me, that sounded like the most amazing thing imaginable. "Well, I'm with you guys, then. I'll be a murderball pro!"

She laughed. "This he says after a single game."

"One that I lost, I might add."

"Exactly."

"I don't know, to be honest. Right now, for me, it's all about finding a normal way to be."

"What does that mean?" I felt her footfalls growing harder, her pace picking up, as the wind wove its wide fingers through my hair.

"Well I got normalcy taken out from under me. So

each day, I wake up, and I'm like: Will this be the one when it comes back? So far – nope. Though I've had my good days."

"Was today a good day?"

"Today's a great day," I said. Present tense, not past.

"Let me ask you a question, Tucker..."

"Shoot."

"Were you ever really normal before?"

"What do you mean?"

"Exactly what I said: Before you got hurt, were you--"

"Of course. I was an ordinary kid. I played sports. I hung with my friends. I chased girls."

"And what do you do right now?"

"Ha! Well, similar stuff, but minus motion in 90 percent of my body..."

"You know what I think, Tucker..."

"I have a feeling you're about to tell me..."

"Yep. I think whatever you thought was so 'normal' before was just a big illusion. No one's normal. Nothing's normal."

"Whatever. You're just taking a position."

"Who's normal, then? Go."

"Kip's normal! Like, totally normal."

"Oh – my – God."

"What??"

"If you think Kip's normal, then you really have no clue what normal is."

My smile was tight against the front of my head. "How is he not normal? He's like the nicest dude."

"Nice, yes, fine. But did you know he often wouldn't sleep before his races?"

"So what? He was anxious. That's normal."

"And that his way of keeping calm was to chat with a portrait of his deceased grandma."

"Okay, so? He missed her..."

"And that the portrait is encased in glass at the bottom of his swimming pool..."

"WHAT??"

"Yeah!"

"WHY??"

"I don't know. She was a champion swimmer or something. So he spent like $10,000 preserving an oil painting inside a pool. Then he goes down there with scuba gear on and has conversations."

I laughed so hard I felt gravity tugging me forward. It took me several moments to recover. When I did, I said, "Okay, so your point is that everyone has quirks?"

"Nuh uh. My point is that normalcy's just a myth. Chase it if you want, but you'll never get there."

* * *

I loved her, then.

Sure, it was euphoric, shallow, chocolate-high-like puppy love, but its precise roots didn't matter. This was my girl right here. It hadn't taken us forever just to weave our way through a conversation. I hadn't had to navigate 18 layers of shyness and mixed messages.

No: Brianna was right here. What I saw was what I got.

How she wasn't already taken was a mystery to me. I gathered from other parts of our conversation that school was her main priority and she wasn't open to distractions. Even the internship had become distracting.

Good news by me: I didn't want anything long-term, either.

Especially, since, judging from what had occurred hours earlier, I was now newly dumped.

I wondered how far my luck would stretch. Could I date this girl? Could we even be close friends? Would this night burn bright in my memory as some lone, random occurrence, never to be repeated again? Did she have nights like this with a lot of guys, or people in general, only to vanish from their lives forever, and leave them with a bright trail of stardust to admire?

"Stop," I said.

I had to be bold.

"What?"

"Stop pushing me."

"Okay." We were on a bridge. She did as requested. I said to her, "Come here."

She circled around to my front. I'd almost forgotten the extent of her beauty. Never before had I gotten such a good look at her. At the snack place, we'd been side-by-side. Now she was right there at 12 o'clock, via a slight upward arc of my gaze.

"What you just said," I said, "was huge to me."

"It was?"

"Totally. But I have a question..."

"Okay..."

"Maybe normal's not the word. But will I ever get back to, like, a flow? Just that feeling that the days go together nicely? That everything's holding at the center?"

"I don't know, Tucker. I mean: I know what you mean. But is that ever how things are, either?"

"They were for me before."

"No they weren't."

"Of course they were!"

"No. They were better for you than they are now, but that's just a comparative assessment."

Damn. She was smart. She slung vocabulary words!

"I'm not sure," I said.

"Think about it, Tucker. Think about the way life works. The nature of it. There are always challenges. Yeah, you might flow for, like, a Saturday afternoon, then by evening you're stressing about this or that."

I sighed. "Maybe."

"Not maybe," she said. "Ever heard of Alan Watts?"

I shook my head.

"He was a Zen philosopher. Super cool. And his writings all came back to the fact that reality isn't fixed. We want it to all be fixed and solid. We want everything to be nice and routine, but somehow it never turns out that way. You know how we get it fixed?"

Again: Me: Shaking my head.

"We die," she said.

I sighed again. "I have a feeling you're probably right."

"You don't have to feel it. It's common sense."

I looked at her. Her eyes caught the moonlight. Before I knew why or how or from where, I heard myself saying to her the words "I'm scared."

She nodded. It took her a moment to absorb this. Then she said, "I'm scared, too."

"Of what?"

"Anything. Everything. The unknown. The future. It's all part of being alive."

"Will you kiss me now?" I asked.

Again: I had no clue how or from where that came. But I certainly knew why.

She smiled. "Sure," she said.

Then she leaned down and kissed me passionately.

* * *

She was wrong about one thing, in regard to her philosophy:

Although normalcy might have been elusive, although that sense of a flow might have been mythological, there was no questioning the fact that love – even in its shallower forms – had a way of layering one's days with excitement.

For the rest of the night, I was going a million miles an hour inside. I wanted to do more with her, ask her for more, see where her limits were, but I'd already bagged an incredible day, and I wasn't about to push my luck.

When she dropped me off at home, it was after 10. I saw that the light in my dad's second-floor office was on. I wondered if he and I would talk. Maybe even apologize. That would be OK by me, but I still hadn't forgotten how he'd driven me out there on the court.

No simple apology could collapse the gap between us.

But that was a problem for another day. For now, I was bidding farewell to Brianna:

"I guess I'll see ya?" I asked.

"Of course. Next game?"

"Sure." I felt a little dejected. I had no clue when the next game was coming, but I supposed it was good that she was open to both of us being there.

She leaned over and kissed me on the cheek. Then killed the engine and stepped outside to get me in.

The entire time she wheeled me over, I felt the aftermath of her kiss buzzing on my cheekbone.

* * *

No words were exchanged with my dad that night.

He stayed in the office for a good long while. From my bedroom, I occasionally heard him clear his throat or turn the pages of a newspaper. I supposed he was still processing his therapy session. Part of me hoped it had been a success. The rest of me got irritated merely picturing the guy's face.

What I'd said to him before hadn't been merely words: I really did wonder what he could say to a therapist that he couldn't say to us. It wasn't like I craved a family that wore their hearts on their sleeves, constantly spilling the contents of their inner worlds to each other, but I did think it was a little strange that his solution to drifting from the rest of us was to establish a secretive relationship with an outside party. Who could know? Maybe he had some dark trauma in his past. Or maybe what had happened to me was gnawing at him in ways I couldn't possibly understand. Regardless, the fact that he now had a shrink didn't give me the feeling that things were moving in a positive direction. Much as I hoped to be wrong, I still sensed the guy slipping down into his own rabbit hole.

As for my other "enemy", Rebecca, I certainly had words with her on that night. I hadn't remotely been expecting as much. It would have been fine by me to doze off with images of Brianna dancing on my brain, but right around midnight, Rebecca texted, asking, "Are u up?"

"Yeah," I wrote back.

She called me right away.

Not exactly subtle there, "girlfriend"...

I answered and paused for a good long while before managing a "Hello."

"Hi," she said.

I breathed in and out. "Why'd you leave?"

"Didn't your brother tell you?"

"He said you said nothing."

"Well...it was Brianna."

"What about her? She was just sitting next to you."

"No. Not just sitting next to me. She said something. Jordan didn't tell you?"

I just remained silent, nostrils flaring like a bull's.

"She, like, totally wouldn't stop talking about what a cutie pie you were and all this crap."

I brightened. I loved her. Brianna, not Rebecca. "So what? She knows you're with me. It was a compliment!"

"She was laying it on a little thick."

"So you get up and leave? During my game? That sucks!"

"I can tell you like her."

Boom.

I couldn't really hide from that one. Right then, for the first time in this whole debacle, I found myself seeing reality from Rebecca's point-of-view. Being threatened by sitting next to Brianna was dumb. Bailing on me during my game – to say nothing of yelling at me before – was awful.

But picking up on the fact that I dug Brianna. Well...

She had a point there.

Still, I wasn't about to cave right away. What good could that possibly do me? No, instead I did what a million-billion guys before me had. It was generic, it was a cliché, but I could not have cared less.

It was still my birth rite.

So I simply lied through my teeth:

"I don't," I said.

"You do. I'm not dumb."

"Look: She's attractive. Duh. But I'm with you. You have to trust me."

Yeah, me – the guy who three hours prior had been kissing Brianna at the park.

It was Rebecca's turn to be silent. It went on for the better part of a minute. When she resurfaced, she said, "I'm sorry for messing up your day."

I sighed. "It's okay," I said, even though it still stung me.

"I don't want to be like this unsupportive girl-friend. But my feelings are locked up in you, Tucker. You have my heart. Do you understand? You drive me...kind of wild."

The heart was a mysterious thing, indeed. 'Cause the moment Rebecca said those words, I loved her all over again.

* * *

I felt bad for cheating, but only somewhat.

Not 'cause I was keen on sneaking around and getting away with it, but 'cause I'd really believed Rebecca was done with me once she left the game. So even if it ever came out one day – which would be a terrible turn of events, indeed – I had a pretty rock solid excuse.

I went to bed thinking about them both.

Both girls had a lot that they could offer. On the physical level, they were even – a tie. Personality-wise, they were from different planets. Rebecca: inward, pensive, shy, slippery. Brianna: outward, bold, argumentative, direct.

I hated and mocked myself for it, but I understood why men so often maintained relationships with more than one woman. In a way, it was balancing. Different partners could appeal to different sides of your personality.

On the other hand, I didn't want to get into the habit of being deceptive. I saw all too clearly how that behavior could rob me of both options pretty quick. Then I'd certainly spiral into a dark place.

So seeing as I was officially with Rebecca, and closer to her by any measure – and seeing as Brianna had only agreed to see me again surrounding a game, which meant that for her kissing someone could have been no big deal – then as far as I was concerned, I was with Rebecca.

Which of course didn't prevent me from thinking

about Brianna every second.

Sigh.

* * *

Though I went into Sunday hoping to avoid any communication with my dad, he put an end to that notion right away, while I was in the kitchen eating some cereal for breakfast.

"I want you to be there. At my arraignment," he said.

Right away, I didn't like the sound of that. "Why?" I asked.

"It's a week from tomorrow," he went on. "I'll take you. You and Jordan and your mother." His breathing was thick and heavy – agitated. As though he himself wasn't sure about this idea, but he had to carry it through for some reason or another.

As for me, I thought it sounded terrible. The arraignment, I understood, wasn't a sentencing or a trial – just a hearing where the judge declared the charges and the parties agreed on how to proceed – but still, the idea of being in a courtroom didn't sit well with me. Particularly a courtroom where my dad was under scrutiny.

No: If you had left it up to me, I would have been as far from that courtroom as humanly possible.

"I have tutoring," I said.

"You can skip it. We'll cancel."

"I need to file an excuse when we cancel."

"So file an excuse, then, Tucker."

"What will I say?"

"The truth!"

We looked at each other. He realized he'd yelled. He cleared his throat and said to me, quieter this time, "The truth."

* * *

"You're kidding," I said to Kip Cruiser on the phone, 10 minutes after my dad's grim invitation. In fact, it had been Kip's call that had saved me from the encounter with my dad. Now I was out in the hallway off the kitchen with my cell phone pressed against my ear.

"No," Kip said, "I'm not kidding. They saw you play on Saturday and they want you there. Can you make it?"

Kip was inviting me to my second official murder-ball game. It was a spinal cord injury charity game. I was the only one from my team they'd asked to come.

"No pressure," Kip said. "It's an exhibition. Just have fun. Like you did on Saturday. I'll be there. Monica. *Brianna...*"

He sprinkled a little bit of music onto that last name.

"Why will you all be there? It's a big deal?"

"Well, no. I mean: Kind of. In terms of building my brand. Hey, um – you sound kind of against it. Am imagining that?"

I breathed. "What time's the game?"

"After school hours: 2:30."

"Hold on."

I held a palm over the phone. "Dad!"

"What?" He was still in the kitchen, downing oatmeal, sounding like a man with a trillion things weighing on his mind.

"What time is court?"

"Why? You have plans, Tucker?"

"What time?!" God, that guy knew the fastest route under my skin.

"1:30. Why?"

I breathed again and went back to Kip: "I can't make it."

"Tucker! How come?" It was the first time I'd ever heard Kip acting vulnerable, let alone annoyed with me.

"This...thing. It's personal."

"You and I don't get personal? Come on, don't hurt my feelings, bro." He attempted a laugh at that point, but it came out weak.

I lowered my voice a few notches and said, "My dad has an issue. He has to be in court and he wants the family there."

"That day?"

"That day."

"Well, um, what time is court?"

ROLLING HOME

* * *

I was a crazy person.

I actually agreed to let Kip Cruiser and his gang pick me up outside the courthouse right when we were done so they could peel through traffic to get me to the charity game. The vibe I got was that if this had involved motorcycle racing, Kip, who'd been a superstar in that world, would have let my participation slide. But since it involved his renewed attempt to conquer murderball, he had to do his damnedest to make it work.

Plus, you know, my ego was involved:

If I was gonna be his star player, I had to do my best to show up and give it my all.

I didn't tell my parents. Didn't make a peep to Jordan, even. As far as they were concerned, as a matter of course, right after court they'd simply drive me home.

Overall, that week I was a quieter-than-usual form of person. Rebecca kept texting and calling, but I kept my distance. When I did reply, I was sure to be warm, but in general I hung up something of an energetic "Do Not Disturb" sign over my world. Even the movie club guys reached out, figuring ample time had passed and it was now appropriate to check in.

It was not.

Truth be told, this whole court thing had me all wound up.

And add to it the pressure of the game right after,

and this was a week I wanted over as soon as possible.

CHAPTER 10

Showing

I n the end, the best part – if you could even call it that – of the week leading up to my dad's day in court was its ability, by way of its sheer suspense, to get me to stop focusing on Brianna. From our Saturday together into the following morning, she'd taken up pretty solid residence in my stream of consciousness, almost like she was a sudden roommate in my psyche. My dad and Kip conspired to put an end to that, even if Kip was, in fact, orchestrating the circumstances by which I'd see her again.

As for my dad, he was a phantom all week. He left once or twice for hours at a stretch. I'd ask my mom if he was at therapy again, and she'd tell me she didn't know. When he came home, I'd expect that familiar barroom stench to be emitting from his body, but he smelled – and seemed – perfectly normal. He'd make light small talk with us for several moments before slipping upstairs to his office and shutting the door.

A man of secrets.

But come the courtroom, his secrets were fated to be revealed...

* * *

Yeah, court was not my favorite place in the world.

It felt like school, only a hundred times more sinister and bureaucratic. It occurred to me, as my mom wheeled me in, that I hadn't been in a government building in better than half a year. The vibe was parallel to that of my school's: linoleum floors, fluorescent lighting, double-paned window glass. It seemed the same group of people had put the two buildings together. The most notable difference, at least at first, was that security had a heck of a time with me at the front entrance. Since my wheelchair's made of metal, I couldn't just pass through the detectors like everyone else. Two guards had to scan me thoroughly, even turning my pants pockets inside out. It was farcical, ridiculous. If *I* was worthy of this much attention, then these guys really didn't have too much to worry about.

When we got into the courtroom, the only seats we could find were halfway to the back. It was crowded. We had no clue when my dad's case number would be called. That put me in a bind as far as Kip was concerned. My pulse-rate increased as I started planning how to word my exit to my family:

"I have to go..."

"Um, I didn't tell you, but I gotta leave..."

"Hey, um, look...I'll explain later...but I gotta get out of here..."

I eyed the clock above the judge's gleaming bald head. It was 20 past one. My dad was hovering over me, my mom, and Jordan. He had a taut man with gleaming eyeglasses at his side. "I'm going up near the front," he whispered.

"Are there seats?" I asked.

"They're coming back from lunch," he whispered back. "My number comes up first."

I buckled with relief. My dad and the man, his attorney, moved toward the front of the room and maintained a standing position just near the barrier between the spectators and the court itself. Within moments, my relief made way for anxiousness. Even though this wasn't about sentencing or studying the case itself, I was still about to witness my dad as a part of "the system." And maybe even learn a thing or two about what he'd done...

I looked around. His "victim", the man he'd punched, didn't seem to be anywhere in sight. Then again, there were well over 80 people in there. Perhaps the guy was hiding out somewhere. I kept my eyes peeled. Leaned into my mom and said, "How long do you think this will take?"

I wasn't thinking about my murderball game.

I was thinking about wanting to feel calm again.

"Two minutes," she said. "They just plead. But your dad wants to make a statement..."

"A statement?" My throat got tight. "About what?"

She didn't answer. The judge's gavel came down. A case number got called, and sure enough it was my dad and his lawyer's cue to step toward the bench. I expected them to sit down behind one of the tables, as another man – the prosecutor – was already sitting down behind one. But instead, my dad and his lawyer walked up to a little podium with a microphone angling up out of it. The judge, sounding like he'd been through this process so many times that he was half-numb to it, asked them, "How do you plead?"

I braced for the sound of my dad's voice, but his lawyer leaned toward the mic: "Not guilty, your honor."

My eyebrows lowered. How were they gonna prove that one? To the best of my knowledge, it was a cold hard fact that my dad had punched the guy!

The judge studied a file laid out before him. His own eyebrows were bending south. I got the sense he was thinking, or reading about, exactly what I was. When he looked back up, his eyes were on the prosecutor: "What say The People in this matter?"

The prosecutor rose and pulled the front of his suit

jacket together, as though he were about to button it, but instead he just let it hang. "Your honor," he said, "the state moves for a misdemeanor charge of Disturbing the Peace, and recommends 12 weeks' community service with a suspended sentence of three years..."

"That means probation," my mom whispered to me. I could hear the tears creeping around from the back of her throat.

But hold on: Things weren't about to go so easily. The judge, I saw, was shaking his head. He said, with no shortage of irritation, "The charge initially filed was felony assault."

Then my dad's attorney spoke up again: "Your honor, my client has a statement he'd like to share..."

"This is not a trial, sir--"

"It's brief your honor. It goes to support the plea arrangement."

The judge cleared his throat. The sound echoed around us. He said, "Go. But I want this brief. We have many cases."

My dad's attorney touched the middle of his back. Shoulders high and tight, my dad stepped toward the microphone. He, like the judge before him, cleared his throat – only unlike the judge, he sounded small and weak.

"Thank you for allowing me a word, your honor."

"Please proceed, Mr. Frost..."

"Your honor, Mr. Davis..." I gathered that was the prosecutor. "...and the people of this state, I'd like to offer an apology for my behavior on the night in question. It is a fact that I did assault Mr. Crenshaw..."

I winced. That didn't sound like the smartest thing to say...

"Though I'd like to share that in the past six months, my life has seen some extraordinary circumstances. My youngest son, Tucker, who I love very much..." He had to take a moment there to pause. "...was shot, accidentally, on a hunting trip. It was my father-in-law who made the error. The bullet entered his neck, and yielded him paralyzed from the neck down, save for the use of his arms, for the rest of his life. After that incident, I admit that I have spent more time than I am comfortable admitting inside of bars...and outside of my home. Avoiding what, for me, has been a crushing turn of fate. Tucker is a great athlete, and a great person. And if I could change places with him, I would do so in a moment..."

The judge sat unmoved, eyebrows in a sustained dive. "Mr. Frost, we're sympathetic to your plight, but as regards to the current felony charges, I'm afraid you're not persuading me to reduce them to a misdemeanor. Indeed, you have just issued a confession."

My breath got caught. My lungs weren't working.

"Sir," said my dad, "if I may say one more thing?"

"Please be swift."

My dad turned back to the sheet of paper on which his statement had been typed. "Mr. Crenshaw, the gentleman whom I struck that night, had been making fun of Tucker prior to our altercation."

My mom looked at me. I looked back. Right away, I could tell she already knew...

My dad went on, "He was bullying me. I was minding my own business. He told me, your honor, that I have a cripple for a son, and said other words that I will not repeat because my son is present here today."

Heads turned. Right then, 80 pairs of eyes were on me. I wasn't very hard to find, on account of my chair and my position near the aisle.

My dad's attorney, no doubt sensing that the judge would say this was all made up, leaned into the mic and shared something else:

"Your honor, last week Mr. Crenshaw signed a sworn statement of his own, verifying what my client is saying, which is that he, in fact, was provoked by way of malicious words, under extraordinary circumstances. We hereby submit the statement and request leniency on the part of the court, consistent with the prosecution's recommendation..."

The attorney had a blue-tinged sheet of paper in his hand. He approached the bench and placed it before the judge. The judge slid reading glasses onto his face and spent several moments reading over the paper. When he came up for air, he kept the glasses on but looked over the glass toward my father:

"Mr. Frost: You put me in mind of Martin Luther King, Jr..."

I blinked. That sounded like a nice thing to say...

The judge went on, "For it was MLK who once said that he would never allow any man to bring him so low as to make him hit somebody..."

"Oh, come on," I whispered, nearly inaudibly. Just the same, my mom reached out and pumped my hand. I got the message: *Be quiet.*

The judge then sealed and parted his lips. "*However*," he went on, making my nerves unwind, "I have never known the experience of having a child hurt in the way your son was. Nor have I known harassment such as that you had endured by Mr. Crenshaw. And the court would like to acknowledge Mr. Crenshaw's candor on this matter..."

I looked around again, but no – he wasn't there.

"Nor, I must say, did Martin Luther King know suffering of this kind, or harassment of this kind..." In a surprising moment, the judge cracked a smile. "So I therefore ignore the prosecution's request..."

"Ignore??" My mom's voice was drenched in panic.

"And," the judge continued, "I hereby drop all charges in this proceeding. Mr. Frost..."

My dad's head was low, his eyes dripping tears.

"...I urge gracefulness on your part. And I trust you can find it without the court's assistance. Don't prove me wrong."

BAM!

The gavel cracked like thunder.

ROLLING HOME

The judge said, "You're free to go."

* * *

I was so dizzy I almost forgot about murderball.

Outside the courthouse, we were a pack of giddy children. Everybody talked at the same time. Everybody repeated things the judge had said. We all agreed it hadn't looked too good for a minute there.

And we all praised my dad for his performance.

At one point, as we neared the curb to cross the street back to the parking lot, my dad and I made eye contact for the first time in a whole long week.

"You did that for me?" I asked him.

Tears lit up his eyes, reflecting the sun. "Of course, kid. And I would again."

Playfully, my mom slapped his arm. "Not so fast, there, Rocky."

We all laughed.

"Come on," my dad said, "let's get lunch. I'm starving."

Jordan, who was loosening his tie, said, "Good idea."

My mom gave a nod.

"I can't go," I muttered.

All eyes were on me.

"Can't go or don't want to?" There he was again: same old dad. Gosh, the guy just had a way of gnawing at me.

I supposed, at that moment, that this would maybe be a lifelong process, learning how to make peace with him.

But even if it took my whole life, I was willing to try.

I told them about my murderball game. In light of our great day in court, I underwent no pain as I shared the word. It was what it was.

And Kip was due any moment.

It took them a moment to absorb what I'd say. No one was angry; they just seemed a little confused. "Why didn't you tell us?" my dad wanted to know.

"I kind of thought maybe you had other things on your mind."

He nodded. Swallowed. Looked at my mom. Said: "Well, looks like we're not going to lunch."

"What do you mean?" I asked him.

And he smiled.

* * *

My family cheered loud and proud that day.

As for my game, it was different from the last one. For whereas the last one had been fueled by anger, this one was fueled almost entirely by joy.

Sure, I had my moments of rage. For example, when a member of the opposing team crushed my thumb pretty good between her chair and mine.

But even then, I had to keep on smiling.

And laughing, at times, as I burned up that court.

Kip could see it, could feel it – I sensed as I played. For the caliber of my game was identical to the caliber of his bike racing: which is to say, fueled by passion. Heart. Soul.

Joy.

It was a blur. I just remember my parents screaming. And Jordan, too – much more than he had the first time. Brianna was there, also, as promised, screaming my name like last time.

And how it lit up my heart to hear that voice.

It was my dad's day, yes, but it was also mine. And I kind of think God set that all up on purpose. Let my dad shine in court; let me shine out on the court.

Even though, unlike my dad had, I managed to lose again.

"Just a charity game," Kip said, ruffling my hair. "Besides," he went on, leaning in toward my ear, "you play like a devil out there."

I smiled at him. We held our eye contact.

Wherever my future was going, this guy was in it. Of that I had no doubt.

Then Brianna was near me, patting my knee. "Hey," she said.

"Hey yourself."

"You played awesome today."

"Thank you. You cheered awesome."

Devil, indeed.

She smiled. Her skin was tinged with pink. Did she

like me? My instincts all fired a Yes. I mean, hey, on a day like that, everything goes your way. Nail 'em in court. Play like a devil. Get the girl after. Go home with a smile.

Only as it turned out, the girl I got wasn't Brianna.

Another hand ruffled my hair. I stretched my neck to turn around, but I only had so much mobility to do so.

Didn't matter. Rebecca stepped in front of me.

"You're here?" I was embarrassed to hear my own voice crack.

She smiled.

"How'd you know?" I asked her.

"I have my ways," she said.

Brianna, I saw, was drifting back toward the crowd. For a moment, I was sad to see her go. Then I looked back at Rebecca, and realized that my happiness about seeing her far outweighed my sadness over not seeing Brianna.

Sometimes life is funny that way.

You need those little moments to get perspective.

* * *

Rebecca drove me home from the game.

It had turned out to be a weird day transportation-wise. Parents drove me to court. Kip drove me from court to the game. Rebecca drove me from the game to home.

ROLLING HOME

I realized, in a pretty efficient manner, how many good people genuinely had my back.

I simply glowed that day. My whole family did. Our victory before the judge had been so strong, so replete with good energy, that it would take a real tragedy to break our stride.

And I kind of trusted that God would go easy on us with that one. At least for now.

Rebecca and I didn't talk about our relationship, even though the topic hung loud in the air. It was right there on the tips of our tongues, but we both knew it was thorny territory, and there was much to say that picking the moment would be important. So instead, I caught her up on my dad. She was as thrilled about the result as I was, and that only made me feel closer to her.

Just the same, I wasn't sure if we were fated to stay together.

With someone like Kip, it was a done deal: I knew he and I had more business together. We were at the ground floor on something big. If not big business-wise, then at least big as an experience to share. And maybe that meant Brianna would be around me, too.

But Rebecca?

It pained my heart to acknowledge, but I kind of felt myself leaning away from her. Happy as I'd been to see her – happy as I'd been to talk to her and not Brianna – I got this haunting sense that I was beginning to understand her nature and function in my life story.

'Cause it's all just one big puzzle, as I'd long understood. Every event, every person and situation, has its perfect place. It simply can't be any other way.

And as I looked at her that day, I got the sense that her place was to save me after my accident, but not necessarily to carry me the rest of the way.

Maybe she wouldn't see it that way. Maybe she looked at me and pictured years of togetherness.

But wheelchair or no wheelchair, I was still a kid. Still had college, or something like it, ahead of me. Wasn't wise to get tied down this early.

Especially not to someone whose purpose might have already been served.

"You saved my life," I said to her, wrapping my hand around hers as we sat in my yard.

Although the view from Grandpa Angus's rooftop was a beauty, I'd always privately maintained that no better view existed in my life than the one from my own backyard. See, the yard arched downward, in a steep hill, about 40 feet from the house's backdoor. But if you sat right at the lip of that hill, and looked out toward the west, where the sun set and where the Pacific wasn't all too far beyond our sight, you saw the most amazing arrangement of homes and yards and streets and trees. A grand painting created by a godly hand, the sight of which always reached real deep inside me and cooled my soul.

That's where Rebecca and I sat, me in my chair, she in one of her own, when we finally got to talking about the two of us.

"That's a nice thing to say," she said to me.

"It's the truth," I told her.

"Well, you saved me, too, Tucker."

"Ha. I doubt it. Saved you from what?"

"From myself. From my insecurity."

I smiled. "I guess that makes us even."

"Ha," she said, echoing me. She then bounced her shoulder off of mine. "Is even good or bad?"

"What do you mean?"

She shrugged. "If we're even, does that mean we're done?"

I looked out toward the magnificent view. Somewhere out there on those streets was Grandpa Angus. Going about his day as best he could. And somewhere out there, in another sense, amid all the winding formations and deep, eternal mysteries, was my future. I squinted a little, as though doing so would make me see it. But I couldn't.

Never had.

'Cause no one can.

I looked over at Rebecca. My beautiful girl. Kept her hand tight inside of mine.

"Rebecca," I said, releasing a great deal of breath. "I don't know."

I kept my eyes off her.

"I just don't know.

ABOUT THE AUTHOR

Austin Charters is a debut Young Adult author who was paralyzed from the chest down in a freak hunting accident at the age of 12. He is now 24 years old and received a bachelor's degree in business administration from Arizona State University. He continues to work toward a master's in communications from the same University.

In his free time, Austin loves to participate in adaptive sports such as: handcycling, water-skiing, skydiving, and off-road sports. He occasionally does motivational speaking and loves to be an inspiration to those who are going through trials of their own.

For more information please visit:
www.c5roller.com

CPSIA information can be obtained
at www.ICGtesting.com
Printed in the USA
BVHW04s1938011018
528967BV00011B/336/P